BUBBLE VALLEY

....

CC CORRY

with Thomas and Taylor Corry

Mothertree Publishing, LLC
FERN PARK, FLORIDA

This book is dedicated to my sons, Thomas and Taylor for staying with me from day one and helping create this story. You truly earned the credit received for this.
I couldn't have asked for better boys.

To my wonder woman, Cindy. Your tireless effort editing this book confirmed what I already knew. There is no other like you. You are my missing-link and the love of my life.

To every wide-eyed child looking for more.

CONTENTS

BUBBLE VALLEY

A WONDERFUL JOURNEY

....

PREFACE

On a cool damp summer morning in 2009 my youngest son, Thomas and I drove to one of our favorite nature retreats just outside of Albany, New York. Though we lived in the area, it was magical to us because we had needed time alone among the purity of nature and its creatures.

As we got out of our car I wondered whether or not my decision to come to the town park was a poor one, because it seemed a storm was coming in. The wind whipped strong all throughout an open field around a large children's playground.

Behind the playground was a deep valley of grass that preceded a path for people to walk while enjoying the parks flora and fauna. After seeing

Thomas' drooping face at the prospects of having to leave the park early, I had an idea to brighten him up.

As a dad who enjoys being a kid with his children, I have a habit of keeping all sorts of fun toys and games in the back of my vehicles. It's just a given. On this day I pulled out my trusty half-gallon container of bubble soap and brought it to the top of one of the smaller metal slides in the playground.

I sat like a goof trying to balance my big bottom on a small metal seat meant for a seven year old and proceeded to create the bubble storm of the century. Over and over I dipped the wand into the soapy liquid and lifted it high in the air, releasing a sea of bubbles down on the grassy valley below me.

Thomas and I watched them sail back and forth like they had a purpose. I saw the effect I was creating and doubled my efforts. The bubbles danced in the valley as Thomas swirled among them. Jumping, running and as happy as I had ever seen him. As he danced with the bubbles I had an image in my mind of another world that would be called Bubble Valley.

After this vision I called him back up the hill and told him of my idea for a story and he was instantly hooked. Like me, Thomas is an avid reader and loved the opportunity to use his imagination.

Over the last six years both of my sons, Taylor and Thomas have helped me develop the characters you are about to read over the next thirteen books. Without their help this book would not have happened and for this reason I have included them as major contributors to this creation.

Bubble Valley is introduced through the eyes of four major characters. Billy Waters, a twelve year old Spanish boy who had the unfortunate luck of growing up in a "Union" prison with his parents, who committed a heinous crime. When Billy's parent's death sentence is carried out he is sent to live with his grandfather and family in Tangerine Park, Florida.

Billy is lost in the world without his parents and the only life he'd ever known until he's introduced to his cousin Manny's secret hide-out and the mysterious Mr. Caytoe.

Ru-Ado is a thirteen foot tall albino Sasquatch inhabiting the land on the outskirts of Mt. Shasta, California with his extended family. Ru-Ado unintentionally causes the death of his father Ado-Han's brother, Sho-Ana-Do, by two local hunters after they squabble about hunting protocol. Ru-Ado is banished from his tribe to find his way in life.

In Bubble Valley we see the world through the eyes of a Bigfoot and my interpretation of what their true history could be. Writing Ru-Ado's character was tough at first because it can be difficult to get into the head of a creature that isn't fully known.

I'm very grateful for the many Bigfoot researchers, internet forum moderators; television and radio programs who have presented their crypto zoological findings for those who want to know more.

Takeshi Nakano, a seventeen year old baseball phenom and only son to Hiro Nakano, New Japan's most gloried player is destined for a job playing World League Baseball until his universe changes over night after an unfortunate encounter that tests him like never before.

Alone and desperate in the forest, he is forced to survive off of the land. Takeshi questions his life and the choices that were made for him and has the opportunity to change everything as long as he has the courage.

Tem is a fifteen foot warrior of the Anak tribe in Bubble Valley. He is the running champion of the Bubble Valley games and pride of his pyramid city in the middle of the Earth. Tem is caught on ego as he chases his grandfather, Ishmael into the unguarded and dangerous forests that surround his ancient society of giants and learns a hard lesson.

Writing this first book took five months of straight work, but only because I had to rewrite the book with every draft. Yesterday's words were meaningless when I knew there was an easier way to present the story.

Though the entire thirteen book series will take me about seven years to write, I promise to keep you gripped on the story and ready for more the entire time.

With this, I release it to you. Enjoy.
C.C. Corry

ONE

....

THE STRANGE CASE OF BILLY WATERS

Captain Greeley barged into Lieutenant Millman's office as soon as the Lieutenant's bottom hit the chair. He was a large burly man who liked to think he was still in the US Cavalry, where he spent his fondest days guarding a squad of secret government helicopters in the middle of the desert.

The Captain never liked to be seen without his Calvary Stetson. No matter where he went, he was not without that ceremonial hat. Though he wasn't a very bright man, he had a great passion for carrying out the orders of his superiors. A passion he expected his subordinates to have as well.

Lieutenant Millman had just taken the first sip of coffee of the day and really just wanted to breathe for a second before starting his job. The shifts were long at the Aurora Family Prison Center and he liked to get coffeed-up as soon he could before going to work. He was about to work his second consecutive twelve-hour shift in a row and needed as much help as he could get. The facility was losing guards every day and he was filling in the gaps of others who had recently quit.

Millman was in his late twenties, but still looked like a fresh cadet. He had short cropped bright red hair and fair skin scattered with brown freckles. His hazel green eyes burned red from exhaustion.

"Lieutenant Millman!" Captain Greeley screamed.

Millman was not expecting this display of anger from the Captain, but was not surprised by it either. He put his coffee down and stood at attention. "Yes, Sir!" said the Lieutenant.

Greeley was a very picky man, but saw that the Lieutenant had shown him an appropriate amount of respect. No one at Aurora really knew what that was from day today because of the Captain's erratic behavior, but it usually meant that you had to leave your brain in your car before punching into work. The prison was located in what used to be called North

Dakota, now only Division Three in what is commonly known as "The Union".

"Do you know why I was promoted to Captain earlier than any other man in the history of this great and gloried facility, Lieutenant Millman?"

Lieutenant Millman took a quick mental survey of the prison and wondered if he worked in the same place. "Another sip of coffee before I had to see this lunatic would have been perfect," he thought, but said, "No, Sir! Would the Captain like to tell me, Sir?"

"Of course, Lieutenant," the Captain said with a sly grin. "I ascended to this rank quckly because I do not waste my time on wonder. I get to work on-time every day and *I get to work!*" he said. The Captain saw the Lieutenant's popping eyes and knew he had his attention at last and softened immediately. "As soon as I go on shift I get to work. There are breaks at appropriate times throughout the day and this is not," he emphasized, "one of those times. Do you understand?"

"Yes, Sir!" Millman said at the top of his lungs. Just wanting this man to get on with it and find someone else to play with. He scanned his mind trying to think what he did to bring the Captain to his office at all. He was a clean officer and treated people with respect. In the six years he worked at the prison he was only reprimanded once, but that was when he first started. He tried to settle himself, but the Captain made him nervous. The Captain smiled to himself and enjoyed the eerie and exaggerated pause between them. "Lieutenant Millman, you have new orders this morning," he said with a smile.

"New orders, Sir?"

"Did I ask you if you had any questions yet?" the Captain snapped.

"No, Sir!"

The Captain smirked and said, "If you'd let me finish, I could tell you that you've been promoted out of laundry room operations and into case work." He paused again and stared at the Lieutenant. "You can speak," he said with petulance in his voice.

"Case work? That's wonderful news, Sir, thank you very much!" the Lieutenant stammered. Millman had applied for the position over a year ago, but hadn't heard a response since he submitted the application and just forgot about it since then. The laundry room operations were typically kept for officers who needed to learn a lesson because of the hot and humid working conditions and Millman had been there for six years. He had recently started to see it as his own personal prison sentence and suddenly loved this loony Captain.

"You're welcome, Lieutenant," he said and took out his personal notebook to read from. "Your first order is to carry out the reassignment of prisoner appendage number zero, six, two, four; William Augustin Waters, Jr., age twelve."

Millman's look of pride and contentment turned to disgust and loathing in a nanosecond. The Captain looked into him, "Do you remember this prisoner appendage?" his smirk returning.

Millman broke eye contact with the Captain for the first time in their conversation, but said nothing. Prisoner appendage was the term used to describe the children of prisoners. The Captain knew the whole uncomfortable story, but didn't press the Lieutenant. "The appendage's father, William Augustin Waters, born September twenty-seventh, nineteen hundred and seventy. Deceased January twenty-eighth, twenty twenty-six. Mother, Constance Maria De Coronado, born March fourteenth, nineteen seventy-two. Deceased January twenty-eighth, twenty twenty-six."

Millman had known the family well and felt a great lump develop in his throat, but looked directly at the Captain, "How would you like this handled, Sir?"

he asked. The Lieutenant wanted to show the Captain that he could handle tough situations with ease, but the Captain was unsure.

"What do you mean, Lieutenant?" his face contorted. "I want it done quickly; now take these orders and get out of here!" the Captain said and held the document out.

Millman saluted and took the paperwork, placing it on his clipboard and ran out of his own office, leaving the Captain behind. The door closed behind him and he hustled down the sterile white hallway towards the exit doors. Even though the walk to the Water's trailer was only sixty seconds away from the main offices of the prison facility the Lieutenant reached for a thick uniform coat on the wall and put it on. He opened the doors, breathed in deeply and braved the cold.

TWO

INTO THE MIDNIGHT AIR

Billy crept out of his bed and walked as quietly as he could to the small bathroom in his family's trailer. He was a small boy for the age of twelve at four feet two inches tall and had dark straight hair, with bangs cut just above his eyebrows. His deep blue eyes were hidden under his blanket, which was draped over his head like an overstuffed robe. Though large and no doubt warm, there were many holes in the old blue cover. "Jeez, it's cold!" he said in a loud whisper as not to wake up his mother. Smoke shot from his mouth and nose every time he breathed.

He didn't know how she was able to hear over his father's monstrous snores, but she always did. He walked through the bathroom door and closed it quietly behind him. Billy went to the bathroom without the use of lights or even having to take his hands out of the blanket. A practice easy to marvel until it was no longer successful.

Once finished, Billy turned around, walked mechanically back to bed and was once again blasted by his father's bear-like snores. He had no idea how his mother was able to sleep next to him, but she always said, "I'm just glad to be able to sleep next to him every night." It bothered Billy a lot because *he* was having trouble falling asleep too.

His mother Connie, always smiling said, "Your father works in the mines all day and is completely exhausted by the time he gets home. The least we could do for his dedication to us is to fall asleep a little earlier than he does. It won't work every time, but at least we won't be un poco loco." They both laughed.

Billy carefully walked back to his room and closed the door. Though this only muffled his father's eruptions it still helped a lot. As he lay back down the heavy whir of the winter wind whipped against the old football stadium dome and made a sound like rolling thunder. Billy lost himself in the noise and sank deep into his mattress, feeling lightness throughout his body. He breathed deep and cast another stream of frozen vapor towards the ceiling.

His body began to shake from the inside out and became paralyzed by fear. No matter how much he tried he could not move. He tried to talk, but all that would come out were low, short bursts of air from his lungs. The struggle within him to move was furious, but he was a prisoner to it.

Something deep inside him said, "Just relax and let it all go." A voice he felt he'd always known soothed his soul. "Just breathe in... and out..."

Billy did as was told without even thinking, breathing deeply. The voice repeated "Relax..." and Billy let the feeling travel through his legs and shoot up his spine like a lightning bolt, finally settling at the base of his skull.

At once it felt like an earthquake had gripped Division Three. Billy felt a minor earthquake a few years back, but it was nowhere as intense as this. He rose out of his body and floated a few feet above, looked down and saw himself sleeping below, "Am I dead?" he thought.

The voice answered as quickly as the thought came. "You never die. You've only changed. Relax," it comforted.

A wave of love passed through him and he lost the last of his concern. What remained was his curiosity. He looked at his little body and saw that he could see through it. "Awesome!" he thought as he looked around his room. Everything looked exactly the same, but the colors were a little different. He couldn't really tell the difference, but it was certainly there.

"What is this place?" he said aloud and began to float upwards towards the ceiling. A minor fear began to creep in again and a small tug pulled in what he thought was his belly, but quickly remembered the voice's soothing words.

"Relax..."

He floated upward and into the ceiling, seeing the layers of plastic, metal and insulation that protected his family from the harsh elements of post-nuclear war. He looked all around the big dome and saw hundreds of small trailers lined up in neat rows all throughout. As he rose higher and higher into the sky the trailers began to look like one of his Lego town constructions.

He smiled as he thought this might be the best moment in his young life, never feeling freer. He stretched his arms and pushed his legs against the air. It almost felt as if he were in a bathtub full of water when he was very young. When he pushed his legs he rose higher and higher, zipping through the dome's enclosure and up into the open air.

He gasped as he saw the moon and the stars for the first time in person and marveled at the size and complexity of colors. It looked so different from the many pictures he had seen in books and videos shown in the prison's school. He rose higher and higher until his cheeks kissed the clouds. He twisted and twirled as he lifted even further and wondered, "Does everyone know how to do this?" and quickly thought of his parents.

"Mom and Dad would *love* this. I wonder if they know how too?" he thought.

At his thought's command he shot back to the ground at a furious rate of speed. Wind pushed against his face as he zoomed towards the Earth below. He came to a complete stop and found himself in a stone courtyard, large enough to fit his entire trailer. Its granite walls were lined with wooden staked torches whose flames grew large with the swirling wind.

A group of soldiers armed with rifles stood at ease near the south wall. The gathering of men was tense, but all clearly focused. Some smoked cigarettes as they stood and others merely looked off into the distance. None of them said a single word.

At the opposite end of the courtyard were two people; one large and hunched over, holding on to the other in a desperate embrace. The smaller of the two was weeping loudly and praying, but Billy couldn't quite make out what she was saying.

Both had large burlap sacks placed around their heads and tied at their necks. Billy didn't know who they were or why they were there, but still felt for them; his heart aching for their pain.

In a far corner of the courtyard he saw a shadow shift, as something tried not to be seen. Billy wasn't afraid as he was a big fan of fiction horror and had been scaring himself silly from the day he learned to read, but certainly didn't want to see it any closer.

He switched his gaze back to the people, now both standing, still holding each other closely. Billy did not like looking at them either, but what was hidden in the shadows made his stomach lurch like never before.

Though unmoving, he heard it breathe; a slow and raspy harsh gurgle of a sound. It seeped from the corner like a wave of evil. In, out, in, out, in, out. The sound kept getting louder and louder in his ears.

Billy thought, "Jeez, just shut up already. I can't hear myself think." He put his hands against his ears and the sound went away. He took his hands away again and the sound was still gone. He tilted his head in wonder.

He looked again at the couple and they were now standing tall, only their heads bowed in submission and saw something familiar about them both; one so large that the smaller of the two had to reach up to hold the taller person's hand.

He heard a noise come from a metal door on the north wall of the courtyard. A large man in a tan uniform similar to that of the soldiers walked in front of the group of men. The only difference in his clothes was his hat and boots. He wore an old-time cowboy hat with a small gold star on the front and black combat boots polished as clear as mirrors.

He walked like a man in charge and the men responded like it. The men who were smoking cigarettes tossed them to the ground and stood at the ready. The other men who seemed lost in space were now peering forward at their leader, waiting for a command. The man scanned the group quickly and saw nothing out of order.

17

He yelled loudly, "Attention!" his voice echoing off of the walls. The soldiers stood rigid and placed their rifles at their sides. The hooded people stood rigid and waited. The woman wept silently to herself.

The soldier with the cowboy hat stood off to the side, out of the way of the men. He raised his right arm and said, "Ready..." The soldiers took up the rifles in their hands. "Aim!" he snarled. The rifles were pointed directly ahead. The soldiers ready for the execution of these two people.

"Oh my God," he thought and was amazed to hear the woman's thoughts at the same time. He heard the desperate prayer of his mother. He shouted, "Mom! Dad!" stunned by the horrible vision in front of him.

In the corner of the courtyard, the shadow's breathing turned from a rasp to a slow chuckle of a laugh, "Ha, ha, ha, ha, ha..." it walked into the wall and out of sight.

The soldier in the cowboy hat lowered his hand and yelled, "Fire!" The look on his face was defiant and proud. His soldiers all fired their rifles at the same time and Billy's parents were dead. Their bodies, once tall and strong fell to the ground hard like two bags of coal.

The ground beneath him began to tremble and Billy heard the slow laugh of the shadow man echo all around him, "Ha, ha, ha, ha, ha..." the sound went on and on.

He screamed out in fear and shot back into his body in an instant. He opened his eyes, looked around and saw the familiar scenery of his bedroom in his family's trailer. He sat up quickly, looked around and sighed in relief. "Oh thank God, it was only a dream." He dropped his head back on the pillow and felt the wetness of sweat saturating his cold pillow.

He turned it over and lay down with his hands behind his head, his damp hair wetting his palms. "Was that *all* a dream? It seemed so real," he said to the empty room.

Unlike a normal dream, he didn't have to think hard about what he just saw. The image of his parents being shot by firing squad was emblazoned in his mind. He remembered the shadow man and thought, "What was that thing?" He was still perplexed by the whole experience. He stayed in bed until he felt the overwhelming need to go to the bathroom again. He sprung out of bed and grabbed his tattered blue blanket, swirling it behind him like a cape. The room felt a bit warmer, but Billy was so small and thin he needed all of the stuffing he could get.

He walked out of his bedroom door like a conquering king, his cape dusting the floor. Light started creeping into the trailer and gave the family's scant furniture an eerie, out of worldly look. Billy took three steps into the room and knew something was horribly wrong.

At first he couldn't place it, looking side to side as if the furniture had been moved. He walked to the trailer's living room window and looked outside. He saw the light was on in the prison's headquarters, but no guards were outside yet. He turned around, staring into the middle of the room and suddenly knew what it was. He didn't hear his father's snoring.

Fear crept into his body all at once, wanting to send him into shock, but his want overwhelmed whatever fear was in him. He forced his feet to walk within an inch to his parent's door and called out, "Mom?" loud enough for her to hear even after her most tiresome day in the hot laundry rooms. He stood as still as he could and listened into their bedroom. Holding his breath just to make sure, but nothing came.

20

He gasped for stale air and thought about calling out again, but did not want to know for sure. He turned around and sank to the ground outside of his parent's door, curling up into the blanket. His entire body was numb.

"Knock, knock, knock!" Three sharp raps came from outside. Billy looked to the door wanting to call out, but couldn't find the words.

"Knock, knock, knock!" The sound came again.

THREE

....

MORNING HUNT

Four large, hairy humanoid creatures walked slowly down the side of the mountain looking for any signs of prey. The largest of the four was blazoned white, with deep red eyes, standing no less than thirteen feet tall. He was all white, except for his vast mane of silver hair around his thick neck and shoulder muscles, making it seem as if he didn't have a neck at all. His chest and stomach muscles were larger and more ripped than the strongest of men. If there was a king of the forest it was he, because no other inhabitant of the woods would seek him as prey.

He roared at the top of his lungs. His monstrous voice taking over the evening air, "Where are the deer? Where are the elk? Where are the boars?" His words came out sounding like a mixture of

Native American and the Japanese languages, but had a style all its own.

A black and graying eleven foot Sasquatch ran over from its forward hunting position and quickly went chest to chest with him. His eyes were furious and ignited with passion. His voice was low, menacing and sarcastic. "We are certainly not going to find them by screaming like humans into the forest. What are you thinking, Ru-Ado? You know we haven't eaten for days and the women and children are surviving almost only on nuts and berries. Anymore yelling like that and you're sure to scare off every remaining animal from here to the Sacred Grounds," he said as his large nostrils flared in the cold, snorting a cloud of smoke.

Ru-Ado expanded his enormous white-haired chest, growled low and exploded; pushing the older Bigfoot off of him. "I know, Sho-Ana-Do! Go back to your position, there is nothing to talk about," Ru-Ado snapped.

Sho-Ana-Do was still upset at his nephew. "Your father, Ado-Han, placed you at rear because you are supposed to be a great hunter, though I don't think he's taught you enough about respect for your elders," he whooped and jumped closer to Ru-Ado, getting face to face.

Ado-Han, a black, twelve foot Sasquatch, left his position behind the point and galloped on all fours to the arguing two. He had a large and silvery mane, very much like Ru-Ado's but it had thinned out over the years. What stood out about his appearance was that he had a large scar on his chest, from a battle long ago. He stood between his brother and son and looked at them stoically.

He leaned into them and said, "I have heard enough today to question both of your positions in this tribe." Ado-Han growled low, but his words were fierce. He showed uncharacteristic anger and the effect on Sho-Ana-Do and Ru-Ado was clear.

They stood at attention to their leader. Not because he inspired fear in them, but because Sasquatches or Zuzuan as they are called in the forest away from the ears of man, live without fear in a land that has no rival and only follow the laws of the Zuzuan warrior.

Ado-Han looked up at Ru-Ado and said, "A leader never forgets his purpose above all things and ours right now is to feed ourselves and the rest of the tribe. Now get back into position." He growled loud enough to send chills up each of their spines. "And don't break ranks again!" he said. From a distance

25

came a sound they all heard at the same time. A warning call came from Tor-Ado, Ru-Ado's younger brother who had taken the point once Ado-Han had left it to chastise Ru-Ado and Sho-Ana-Do.

"Hoot, Hoot! Hoot, Hoot!" came an owl call from Tor-Ado.

The three massive Sasquatches stood frozen and waited for the next call that would tell them if they should expect a fight or coordinates on spotted prey. First came the lonely song of a male mockingbird. A signal that told them an elk was in play. They listened intently as the next one would tell them which direction the elk was heading by knocking on a tree with a log.

A series of sharp knocks came from the bottom of the hill.

Ru-Ado looked up at the moon and saw it large and true. He knew the elk was coming his way. All they needed to do was wait patiently and pounce when the moment was right. He knew what would happen if the elk got one of his antlers into him and he would not let that happen.

Ru-Ado listened closely. "Get behind the trees," he whispered, "Quietly." His words were almost too low for anyone to hear.

Sho-Ana-Do and Ado-Han cucked behind a group of tall and tender Blue Oak saplings, but not before Sho-Ana-Do got in another verbal jab on Ru-Ado, "Look whose asking for quiet?' he said with sarcastic disdain.

Ado-Han looked at Sho-Ana-Do hard and grunted, "Enough already." He had heard enough of his brother's negativity.

Sho-Ana-Do looked upset, but didn't say anything more. He kneeled on the ground and waited, but his leg shook with emotion. Sho-Ana-Do was angry at many things.

In the last five years alone he lost his father and mother to illness. He knew they were old, but not that old. Many zuzuans live for a hundred winters if they live in a bountiful part of the forest, but Sho-Ana-Do's parents were not that lucky. After the great flash in the sky, many of the zuzuans left the land of their forefathers to follow the prey, but his parents were held to it. In just seven moons their hair began to fall out in big patches. Making the once majestic two look like they had mange. Then they just stopped eating altogether, eventually finding solace in the thick of the woods to die in peace, knowing they would never reach the Sacred Grounds on their own.

27

Sho-Ana-Do also lost his wife and daughter only five full moons ago, but this time it was to human hunters. He and his family were looking to swipe a calf from a farmer's herd, but were ambushed by the hunters. The farmers had been weary to the many attempts at their livestock over the last few years and scheduled patrols among neighbors. Sho-Ana-Do watched from the tree line as the group of men fired the thunder-sticks at his family. After carrying them both to the Sacred Grounds he joined up with his brother, Ado-Han's tribe. His emotions ran high because he did not know what else to do. Sho-Ana-Do waited for the elk and growled under his breath.

Ado-Han looked at his brother's scowling face and knew he had to be ready for anything. Out of a dead silence came the call. The low screech of a waiting falcon rang through the air. Normally a call that would send any small animal in the forest into the nearest safe zone, but for a bull elk it was just another bird.

Both Sho-Ana-Do and Ado-Han perked and readied for the chase. Another call came louder, as if it were hovering over its prey and ready to swoop. This was the indicator to all that their prey was drawing close. They would hold still and be ready to pounce.

Sho-Ana-Do twitched and snorted a little too loudly. He shifted his arms and readied to launch. Ado-Han whispered to his brother, "What do you think you're doing? Be still, you'll be eating soon," he chastised.

Sho-Ana-Do heard his brother, but didn't respond. He sniffed the wind and knew the elk was only fifteen feet away. His stomach lurched and the need to eat made him tear off into the forest ahead of the call to attack, a direct violation of their initial agreement. One that was planned out in detail by Ru-Ado and approved by Ado-Han.

Ado-Han growled to himself and chased after his brother, knowing that his sons would not be ready. The elk heard Sho-Ana-Do's early advances and quickly darted off at full speed on a collision course with Ru-Ado. Ru-Ado heard the elk coming right at him and knew that Sho-Ana-Do had jumped the gun. He grimaced at the lack of respect and what it could potentially mean, but focused on catching breakfast first.

He never liked having to tackle down a speeding elk, but sometimes there was no other way. He steadied himself just long enough for the animal to come blaring through the trees directly in front of him.

29

The elk's eyes were wild with the chase when it saw Ru-Ado, but its momentum was too much for the big buck. It barreled right into great white beast who grabbed the elk by its wide horns and twisted its neck, quick and hard. Ru-Ado heard the beast's neck snap and let it fall to the ground. He looked at the food beneath him and wanted to be thankful for the needed meal, but could only stew in anger at his uncle's careless move.

Right behind the elk, Sho-Ana-Do came in hard and fast. He saw Ru-Ado standing over the prey, glaring at him in contempt. Sho-Ana-Do saw Ru-Ado's hatred for him and knew that he had to put this young warrior in his place. He roared thunderously and charged the much bigger Ru-Ado.

The two giant zuzuans clashed in battle and beat on each other mercilessly. Ado-Han arrived a few seconds later, followed by his younger son, Tor-Ado. They saw Ru-Ado and Sho-Ana-Do going blow for blow. Sho-Ana-Do tried mightily, but was easily outmatched by Ru-Ado.

Though fights within Zuzuan Tribes were not uncommon, they were not common in Ado-Han's tribe. The normally reserved leader let out a roar that made every bird in the forest within a mile from them stand still in fear. The land was quiet except for the two giant zuzuan warriors beating great hairy fists upon one another.

Ru-Ado's eye caught his father's and knew he was wrong. He jumped high in the air and grasped for a heavy limb to pull him up, "Enough, uncle! I have no wish to fight you," he barked.

Sho-Ana-Do saw his nephew's leap as weakness and hurled his muscular body upward and swiped at the branch under Ru-Ado's feet. Ru-Ado somersaulted to the ground a half-second before the branch was torn from the tree by a great blow.

Ru-Ado jumped to another tree close by, but this time slapping Sho-Ana-Do square in the face on his way up. The loud clap rang out and echoed in the valley. If he couldn't stop his uncle from fighting with words, he would do it by embarrassing him in front of his father and brother.

Sho-Ana-Do screamed in fury and jumped at Ru-Ado again. At eleven feet tall and six-hundred pounds, Sho-Ana-Do would be a nightmare to any other creature in the woods, but to Ru-Ado, he was just a nuisance.

Each time Sho-Ana-Do attempted to knock him down, Ru-Ado easily jumped away and smacked Sho-

Ana-Do's head with his huge, hairy white hands. Ru-Ado did not want to hurt his uncle, but also needed to make sure he knew that he was not going to be bullied by anyone.

Each slap drove Sho-Ana-Do more and more insane with rage. He tried to lunge one more time and was again smacked hard, this time on his brow. The blow stung him hard. He grabbed his head in pain and took a knee to the ground as not to fall.

He knew he was bested and roared in frustration. He stormed off into the thicket, knocking down every tree in his path as if they were matchsticks. Their sound littered the air and lessened as Sho-Ana-Do's distance from them became greater.

Ru-Ado jumped down to the ground with a great thud and faced his father and brother. Ado-Han looked at his son with disappointment, but did not say anything about what just happened. He looked back to Tor-Ado who was guarding the elk. "Take the elk back to the camp. We are going after Sho-Ana-Do before he does anything foolish," he ordered.

"Yes, Father, right away." Tor-Ado, a brown, ten foot Sasquatch with deep set black eyes was a dutiful son and glad to show his willingness to help whenever he could. He looked at the dead elk with hungry eyes, but bent down and heaved the animal over his shoulder. He walked slowly but surely back from the direction they all had come.

Ru-Ado tried to apologize, "Father..." he pleaded.

"Not now, we will talk about this later," Ado-Han said, brushing off his son's attempt at an apology. He looked at him in the eyes and said, "I thought you would have remembered that your uncle has lost everyone he loves in the forest just a short time ago. If you are to be the zuzuan you seek to be, you must learn compassion." His voice was tired and drawn.

Ru-Ado stood dazed by his father's words, but knew he was right as well. Ado-Han walked quickly in the path of the recently felled trees. Ru-Ado tried to forget his anger and followed behind his father. They listened closely for any sign of Sho-Ana-Do, but heard the only thing in the woods that gave them pause; humans.

Ado-Han and Ru-Ado heard one talking loudly from behind the trees just fifty feet ahead of them. "Did you see the size of that dang Sasquatch?!" said the first one.

"Did I see it? *Jesus*, Willie, I'm standing right next to you! Glad we got the fifty-cal out here today," said the second human.

"That don't mean nothing, these things are monsters, Man. Lock and load," said Willie.

Ado-Han looked back to Ru-Ado with fear in his eyes. A sight his son had never seen. "Thunder-sticks. They have thunder-sticks. Be silent," his voice was barely a whisper, but still enough for Ru-Ado to understand clearly. He had heard his father's tales about when he was younger and foolish.

He and his tribe were hungry and began taking chickens from a human's ranch to feed them all. One night, just after a kill he was confronted by a human who shot thunder from a stick as shiny as the noon sun. His cousin charged the human, but was struck down soon after.

They heard them call out again, "Did you see it?" one of the humans said, and heard Sho-Ana-Do making his move to them. The angered zuzuan sought to show these intruders a lesson.

"Uncle, no, they have thunder-sticks!" Ru-Ado called out.

Sho-Ana-Do bellowed his death call and charged the humans. His booming voice demanded attention.

Ru-Ado and Ado-Han heard, "Watch out Darrel, them trees are falling everywhere! There it is!" Willie hollered.

"Fire!" Darrel shouted and they both unleashed a storm of bullets into Sho-Ana-Do's humongous body. He cried out as he fell and yelled, "Ru-Ado!" His body was limp and without life. Sho-Ana-Do had gone back to the Earth.

"Whoo-hoo! We got it!" sang Willie.

"*Holy Christmas*, I thought that bad-boy was gonna kill us both dead-on the spot," said Darrel.

Ru-Ado saw them stand on Sho-Ana-Do's bloody corpse and laugh in excitement. He crouched low and was ready to spring on them. He could take them out in less than a minute, thunder-sticks or not.

Ado-Han grabbed his shoulder and whispered gutturally, "You will not kill the humans. My brother was angry and foolish. There is nothing we can do now." His eyes were focused on the humans.

Ru-Ado looked back. "But, Father... How could we let them do that to him?" he questioned.

Ado-Han looked stern, but gentle. "He is not in that body. He is with his family. I will wait until they have gone and bring his body to the Sacred Grounds. You, will have to leave the tribe," he said, stern but sad.

"Father? What? Leave the tribe? Why?" he pleaded.

"Your uncle was a fool, but he was right. Though you are a skilled warrior, you still lack the tools it takes to become a leader. You must go out on your own and find your reason for walking the Earth. This is the only way," he said as a father and friend.

Ru-Ado, still pent up with anger and frustration burst out at his father, "I am forever sorry for Sho-Ana-Do's death, but I don't agree with you. I am a great leader now and I will prove it to you one day," he said, got up without care about the hunters and quickly walked away from his father.

Darrel spoke up, "Did you hear that?" and put a cupped hand to his ear, but Ru-Ado was gone. He navigated the trees with the confidence of someone who knew every step of the land, but for the first time like a zuzuan without a home.

FOUR

....

TAKESHI NAKANO

Takeshi stepped into the batter's box from the left side. He was learning how to be a switch-hitter and had spent the good part of a month working on his new stance and learning to feel comfortable with the bat in his hands from that side of the plate.

He adjusted his feet so they were no more than a shoulder width apart and crouched slightly. He waved his bat back and forth, finding the rhythm. Once comfortable he brought the bat back to rest, suspended just above his left shoulder. He wagged his bottom just a bit and felt at ease.

In came the pitch from his batting practice pitcher, straight and fast. Right down the plate. Takeshi saw the ball spinning towards him and waited hungrily. He swung and the ball met the bat squarely, sending the orb back over the former World League pitcher and into the mesh fence above him.

The ball sunk into the fabric, rolled down onto the soil and over to a scattered mess of baseballs.

"Good, again!" came from Takeshi's hitting coach, Brian Mattingly, former player in the World League and grandson to Don Mattingly; former New York Yankee and Manager of the Los Angeles Dodgers.

Takeshi revered his coach higher than any other for many reasons, but saw Don Mattingly as his baseball hero, a model to follow and find true perfection in his game. He knew that same quality transferred to his coach.

Another pitch came sailing in; just as hard, just as fast, but curved into him. Takeshi kept his hands back and tucked his shoulder in as he swung his bat forward. The ball met the bat just over the label, sending the ball high above his head and behind him. The ball met the mesh and rolled to the ground, landing with a soft bounce; a lonely soldier.

"OK, that's it for now, Takeshi, you did great! Don't let that last swing distract you, you're just getting tired," the coach said as he looked at his watch. "Wow, we've been here for three hours, you *better* be tired," he said and smiled as he patted Takeshi on the back. Takeshi was silent and nodded respectfully to his coach.

"Go take a shower and get some extra rest tonight. Tomorrow morning we meet with the scouts from the Giants and the Yankees." He had a smile in his eyes that said, "I believe in you".

Takeshi smiled at his coach and said, "Yes, Sir, I will!" He looked to the ground and walked back to his house a few hundred feet behind the enormous baseball complex his father had bu lt for him just after he was born. He replayed the scene over and over in his head, wishing he could have another chance at that last swing.

Takeshi Nakano wanted nothing more for his life than to be the best professional baseball player to ever wear cleats. Quite a tall task for any one person, but for Takeshi there was no alternative. He had no choice but to aim as high as he did simply for one reason. He was the only son of New Japan's most notable baseball figure of all time; Hiro Nakano.

Once his father retired from World League Baseball, he moved his entire family to the San Francisco area in California to train his son full-time, but was soon offered the position of batting coach for the San Francisco Giants. Though he initially protested, his family insisted, knowing his true feelings for the game of baseball.

Once he finally accepted the job, he was always on the road with the team, leaving Takeshi in the care of his many personal trainers and staff of the Nakano family. His wife and daughter lived the life of privileged people outside of the cloud of dismay that fell upon the rest of the world. Their travels were followed by millions of Hiro's fans. They were the queen and princess of baseball, enjoying the riches of the king.

Though Takeshi was left alone with his father's staff he didn't mind. He never understood his family's way of living and tried hard not to care about it as he put his daily efforts in training.

Unfortunately, Takeshi's family found tragedy early one spring morning and everything changed, for a while. His mother and sister were flying to Hawaii from New Japan to spend a week of shopping, eating and seeing the sights, but a freak thunderstorm sent their small private jet into the ocean. The plane was found several days later, but their bodies were never found.

After the memorial service and funeral Hiro decided to re-retire from his duties to World League Baseball and dedicate himself full-time to his only remaining family member, his beloved son and protégé to his baseball legacy.

At first Takeshi loved the consistent attention his father gave him as it was the only he had received in his life to date. It was a dream-come-true to be able to get to know his father, but that soon changed when his father took the role of master.

At the time Takeshi was only fifteen years old and still developing his love for the game. It was hard to see the fun in all the preparation required just to be able to play on a high level with others, when all he wanted to do was relax a little and watch anime.

Before his father took over he was able to still find moments to goof-off from time to time, but now it seemed his father would never leave him alone. Every second of his day was planned and scheduled very carefully.

Luckily for Takeshi, his father realized that he could not stay away from world competition after he was offered the position of General Manager for the San Francisco Giants, the same team that he previously held the job of batting coach.

Hiro was honored at the respect he was given to run their baseball operations and saw it as another feather in his cap. It had always been his ultimate goal to own a professional team, with his son Takeshi, as its star player.

Hiro apologized to his son after he accepted the position and told him, "It has been wonderful training you for these last months, but I have hired a new training team to take you to your next level of mastery." His words came out in rapid fire as he was trying to avoid any emotion. "I will expect you to work harder than ever as I have great plans for you," he said. For the first time in a long time he rubbed his son's head and smiled wide. "One day, the name Takeshi Nakano will be the most famous in the world and *I* am creating him," he laughed a little and walked out of the room, not saying another word to his son.

That night he left to meet the Giants in West Korea and did not see his son for another six months. Their only contact was a weekly video conference call that lasted no more than five minutes.

Takeshi said nothing to his father, but was glad to be left on his own. He was able to be his own man and think about what he would want to do if he didn't have to play baseball. He wanted to miss his mother and sister, but they never showed any real interest in him. It was easier to lose himself in his work.

The best part of being left a one for Takeshi was that he was able to explore the forest that surrounded his house on a rural piece of property about ten miles from the base of Mount Shasta.

Hiro did not like his son going into the woods alone and even went as far as forbidding him from doing so unless he was with one of his staff or trainers.

Luckily for Takeshi they all spent the holidays with their own families. They felt bad that he was going to be alone, but Takeshi was a simple boy with simple needs. He was glad they were gone. The time he spent by himself would be the best in his life and he knew it.

Takeshi loved the privacy and would spend much of his time shooting targets with a gun behind his home. Since his father taught him how to shoot a pistol at the age of nine, Takeshi had no problem carrying a firearm into the woods for protection. Though he always felt comfortable in the forest, he knew there were creatures out there bigger and badder than him.

Takeshi's main reason for going into the woods was because he loved the peace it provided. Peace from everything the outside world had to offer. He loved to walk through the carved paths and just think about the people before him who also sought the same thing in life; mastery in his chosen craft. Baseball was an obsession for his father, but for Takeshi, it was just another means to seek perfection in his world.

He was grateful for his father's diligence in picking out the best tutors in world history and physics, who taught him about the world he lived in and how it worked. It was rare to see such a young man with so much knowledge, but Takeshi had one quality that his father agreed was superior to all others, his ability to be quiet.

From an early age he would repeat over and over to his son, "Keep your thoughts and opinions to yourself. If you are going to master your world you are going to have to march to the beat of your own masterful drum." Takeshi had learned the lesson early and made it who he was as a young man.

Because of his inclination to silence he was able see everything without interaction and for that reason he was able to find satori, which is a state of

46

mind that all of the great Zen Masters have spoken; the space in time where everything doesn't matter, but you and what you are doing.

By understanding this, Takeshi was able to focus to the point where he could easily shoot at any target and hit it flush-on every time. It was also the reason he was able to see the curve on a baseball coming off of a pitcher's fingers and to use the balls curve in order to hit it squarely. These small things all meant so much and he knew it.

On a wet morning just after Takeshi's seventeenth birthday in late November, his coaching staff and house servants left for the Thanksgiving holidays with their families and Takeshi bundled up for a peaceful exertion into the forest where he would run on the trails to get some extra training in.

As the last staff member drove out of the family's mile-long drive way Takeshi finally began to relax. He took a long bath and dressed for a short run in the woods. He left the house without a phone or weapon as they would only slow him down. He would be home within two hours and had no cares in the world.

Takeshi stretched as he walked, feeling his muscles loosening and ready for work. He tested the ground out for running by taking a short sprint ahead. If the ground was too slippery he would just walk and enjoy the day, but the ground was manageable for him. He'd run on ground that had small patches of ice and just avoided the rough spots. Takeshi took off into the woods feeling free and strong. The cold wind felt wonderful on his face as his body stayed warm from the exercise.

He picked up the pace and ran quickly through the trees with the ease of a fox. His feet were light and nimble, each step carefully planned. He ran down a long steep slope and was just about to let loose into a full sprint down the hill when Takeshi slipped on a wet patch of leaves and lost his balance.

He fell face forward down the hill on his stomach and rolled onto his bottom for a short distance before getting turned over again by the force of inertia, rolling head over feet. At the bottom of the hill Takeshi saw a root hanging out of the ground and reached for it, but it was slimy with dirt and muck. The young baseball star to-be fell into a deep and ancient ravine, just missing a narrow wooden bridge used to cross the opening in the ground. His body crashed hard on a bed of moss and fallen branches at the bottom and Takeshi didn't move a muscle.

The sign reads: WELCOME TO CORONADO'S GOLDEN ORANGES

FIVE

....

THE UNFAMILIAR ROAD
HOME

Billy sat in shock in the back of an old Greyhound bus and cried on and off for two entire days. Even though he had never been on the open road he had no interest in looking out of the dirty window to the left of him. When he did manage to take a peek at the landscape outside the bus, everything seemed too quiet. In the few movies he was able to watch over the years that were *not* meant for children, he saw a busy world. Thousands of cars could populate any street at any time of the day, with people walking all over the place.

Billy heard stories of the war that took place just before he was born and knew of the destruction that came out of it. His mother and father would spend many nights telling him about their childhoods and how the country used to be. Billy heard their words, but he would never be able to understand. Until now, he lived his entire life in jail with his parents, under the close supervision of the prison's guards. He knew only what *they* wanted him to know.

He looked at the vacant parking lot called America and felt nothing for it. The world outside the Greyhound bus was empty, but that was nothing compared to what he felt in his heart. He was hollow. A boy missing the main ingredients of his life and there was nothing he could do about it.

He knew what his parents did to wind up in jail until the prison officials decided to take their lives, but that didn't make Billy feel any better about it. They were only two teenage kids when they decided to revenge the murder of Billy's Uncle Manny, who was in the wrong place at the wrong time. Their vindication against the local police who committed the murder was only supposed to be a prank against an ever increasing local police force, but turned to murder when the make-shift bomb they planted inside a mailbox just outside the local police station sent metal fragments everywhere and killed ten people. All of whom were police officers, on and off duty.

Billy ran his finger over the dirty window, spelled "I love you mom and dad", and curled up into his bag of clothes and cried until he fell asleep.

The next morning Billy woke up and saw a sign on the side of the road that read, "Welcome to Blossom County, Florida" and knew he was getting close. The ache in his heart was replaced by a knot in his stomach as the anxiety of meeting family he never met built up in him.

In a few minutes the bus came to stop at a boarded-up bus station. Many of the windows were broken and birds perched on the leaf-covered windowsills. Billy wondered when the last time a bus had actually come into this particular station.

The bus driver turned to Billy, the sole remaining passenger and said, "All right kid, time to get out. It's the end of the ride." He said in the tone of a Carney. He was a heavy-set balding man with a big bulbous nose that seemed to always stay red. When he faced the boy, long wisps of greasy brown hair fell into his foggy eyes. Billy got out of his seat, grabbed his bag and walked down the long isle to doors leading him to a future unknown.

As Billy was about to exit the bus he looked at the driver and saw a bottle tucked under his leg. He nodded to the driver and didn't say a word as he stepped down the buses stairs and onto the cracked sidewalk outside of the station. As soon as Billy got off the bus, he was greeted to Florida by the power of the sun.

The heat was so suffocating that it nearly stole his breath away and the brilliant sun caused him to shield his eyes with his hands and run towards the decrepit building for some shade. Once protected, he looked up at the station's awning and saw large spider webs everywhere. This made him feel very vulnerable and out of place simply because he didn't know how to react to this new environment. Beads of sweat magically appeared all over his head, collected at the tip of his little nose and dripped to the ground. Billy wiped his head and watched a small puddle growing next to his old sneakers.

On a termite-infested windowsill stood a tiny brown lizard who puffed out a bright orange pouch towards Billy and he backed off to give the little creature some space.

As if to say, "You can't come back in here," the Greyhound bus started up again and drove slowly past him, which gave him a brief moment of relief from the blazing sun. Billy watched the bus accelerate down the road and leave him and the little brown lizard in a cloud of thick smoke.

Billy coughed and waved the fog away as the sun took over everything once again. He shaded his eyes and spoke to the unmoving reptile, "I wonder who's going to come get me?" he questioned. The little creature just continued to expand and contract his orange pouch, hoping Billy would eventually get the picture.

Billy's mother had mentioned her family in the past, but he had no real reference of things. There were no faces to go along with her stories.

"Hola!" came a sweet and loving voice hidden by the sunlight. "Is that you, Billy?" she sang.

He knew that voice and thought, "Could it be?" as tears welled in his eyes again. Billy took his hands down and saw the silhouetted woman stand in front of him with a huge smile.

"My God, you *are* my sister's boy," the short slender woman with long flowing black hair said and hugged him deeply. She cried and laughed at the same time. She looked into his face and saw his pain and confusion. "My poor little bird, what you have had to go through," she said as tears streamed down her face and onto his head. Billy let himself be washed by her love. This was his Aunt Maria, his mother's younger sister.

She held the embrace for a long time, knowing his need. "Come on sweet heart, I'm gonna take you home. Wait until you meet your cousins, you are going to be best friends fast."

She took his hand and walked him to her waiting truck. Billy smiled. She opened the door for him and closed it behind him once he pulled himself up and into the white, but mostly rusted vehicle. Billy looked at the inside and studied the different knobs and gauges.

"I know it's a piece of junk, but it works," she said with a laugh.

Billy finally spoke up to his aunt, "I don't think it's a piece of junk, I've just never been in a truck before," he said with honesty.

Maria was surprised, but quickly remembered. "Oh... I didn't know," she paused. "Did they treat you good there?" asking a tough question.

"Where?"

"In the... the..." Maria struggled for the right words.

"The jail?" he asked.

Maria finally managed, "Yeah, that place," in a soft evasive tone.

Billy looked up to think and saw torn pieces of blue fabric hanging down from the truck's ceiling. "Well, they didn't treat me bad. My..." his eyes welled-up and was able to finish his sentence "...mom protected me a lot." He wanted to cry, but held it back.

Maria knew it was too early for any more questions, reached over and gave him another long hug. She pulled back after a while and said, "Enough talk of yesterday or any other day before it. From now on all we are going to talk about is the future and happy times, OK?" she said through held back tears of her own.

Billy smiled tightly and nodded his head and said, "OK," but he knew it wouldn't be so easy.

Maria turned the key in the ignition and the old Ford started up with ease. The engine revved slightly for a minute and then settled in. She put the truck into drive and traveled down the same road as the previously departed bus.

Billy looked at the land and was startled at the difference from what he saw from the road. His parents had told him about the orchards, but the sight of thousands of orange trees lined in rows as far as his eyes could see was hard to imagine until you were right up in them. He smelled deeply and breathed in the sweetness from every open blossom. He closed his eyes and let himself get taken with it.

"It's pretty amazing, huh?" Maria said with a knowing smile. "When I was a little girl, I would love to just sit in the middle of my father's orchard and absorb it all in. I loved being in the middle of nature. Just listening to the birds on the trees and the sound of the wind. And on the rainy days in the summer, you could hear every frog in the neighborhood coming out to talk with each other." The sweet reminiscence made what she had to say next a little easier. She let a few moments pass before saying, "Billy, did your mother ever tell you about your Grandfather, Don Eduardo?"

Billy looked over to her, squinting as he thought. "Yeah... she said that he was very angry with her for what she and my father did to go to jail, but... she really didn't say much more." He paused for a moment and said, "It made her too sad."

"Hmm... I don't know how to say this, but your grandfather is a very proud man, with very firm beliefs. The anger he felt for your parents hasn't gone away at all. He just doesn't know how to forgive," she said.

58

Billy looked at her curiously and said, "What does that mean?" His voice was a little shaky.

"It means that he doesn't want to see you when you come to the orchard to live with us," Maria said while keeping her eyes on the road to avoid seeing the pain in her nephew's face. Billy sat stunned and silent.

Maria continued, "You're going to stay with me and my family in our house in the middle of the orchard. It's our job to take care of it for the family. Don Eduardo is an old man and can't take care of it any more on his own. He lives in a house in the back of the orchard; far away from all of us. He likes to keep to himself," she continued nervously. "I do go see him every few days to clean the house and bring him groceries, but that's pretty much it." She took a quick glance at him and turned back to the road.

Billy spoke up with more strength than he expected. "Don't worry Aunt Maria, I have you and I'm happy." She turned to him again, this time with a big smile, "Yes you do, my little one. I will love you like my own. All will be well, no worries," she said and turned the truck onto an old dirt road. They passed a wooden sign that read in big orange letters "Welcome to Coronado's Golden Oranges".

"This is it?" asked Billy.

"It sure is." She took one hand off of the steering wheel and waved it in one grand sweep and smiled bitterly. "All of this used to be ours, today we just run it. The government owns everything, but..." she quickly changed her tune, "many others aren't so lucky," her voice sweet and sad.

"How do you mean?" Billy was curious.

"After..." she stumbled briefly and recovered, "your mother went away everything changed. First here and then everywhere," she trailed off.

"How so?" asked Billy.

Maria hesitated briefly then said, "The Army came in and took over everything. There's really no other way to say it." She drove slowly down the long dirt road and stared off into the distance. "One morning a soldier came to your grandfather's door and handed him a piece of paper that said we no longer owned the orchard. Don Eduardo tried to protest, but had no more heart for fighting after your Uncle Manny died," she paused again. "He had a stroke soon after that and spends most of these days on his front porch looking into the orchard. When he's not in a world of his own, he's angry at everyone," she said as she looked at him. "It's not just you, Billy. Your grandfather is lost and I don't think we'll ever find him," she said and turned the truck down a much narrower dirt road.

Billy looked out of his window and said, "I'm sad for him," but his voice indicated otherwise.

The truck rolled onto a gravel driveway and up to an old peeling whitewashed farmhouse. Though it was standing well, Billy could see that it had been around for over a hundred years. The more he kept looking, the more odd the house began to look. He cantered his head to the side and tried to figure it out.

Maria saw his face and let out a big laugh. Her smile reached from ear to ear. "You are so cute!" she said, looking at him and Billy reddened with embarrassment. "The house was originally very small when it was built in eighteen seventy-eight by my great-grandfather, but it was more like a cabin back then. Once his family began to grow, so did the house. It may not be a palace, but it's ours, for now," she said, a little sad.

Billy cocked his head when she said those last few words, but didn't say anything. He could tell that his aunt was having a hard time saying all of this for him.

Maria turned off the ignition and got out of the truck. Billy followed with his bag in hand. Once Maria

61

turned the handle to the front door and opened it wide, a large cacophony of sound filled the air.

"Surprise! Welcome home, Billy!" came a chorus from the kitchen.

Maria looked down to Billy who was beaming. "This is your family, Billy! Welcome home," she said with happy tears running down her face.

Billy looked at them all in wonder and gratitude. His eyes glassed-over and gave them a tight smile, as not to openly weep in front of so many people.

"Thanks," was all he could manage to say, but felt a whole lot more inside.

A boy about Billy's age walked up to him with his hand extended. "Hiya, Billy, I'm Manny." He was taller than Billy by a good five inches, but looked like he could be his brother, except for his eyes which were dark brown.

He looked at his younger twin sisters who were still jumping up and down with excitement. "And these are the blunder twins, Elsie and Katerina," he said and crinkled his face as to make fun.

"Hey, we're not twins, we're one year apart!" said two pretty girls who looked like miniature versions of the miniature Maria. They both wore matching pink-polka-dot sundresses and yellow ribbons in their hair. "Momma, what does blunder mean?" said Katerina, the younger and more curious of the two.

Maria ignored her younger daughter's question and looked cross at her son. "Manny! If you can't speak nice about your sisters then don't speak at all," she said in a stern voice.

Manny shrugged it off. "Fine. No problem," he said and smiled as he looked to his mother. "I can do that!" trying not to rile her. He looked to Billy and took his cousin's hand, "Come on, let's get out of here! Let me show you the orchard."

Maria looked hard at her son, "Billy needs to have rest after such a long ride. Don't push him so soon!" she said.

Billy spoke up. "Aunt Maria, I slept on the bus. I'm OK. I want to see the trees," he said with longing.

Maria grinned at her nephew and was affected by his sincerity. "OK, but not too long. I'm going to make you a big welcome lunch," she looked to Manny. "Make sure you're back in an hour," she said and gave him a look that told him that she meant business.

"OK, mom, no problem. I just want to show him my secret spot," he said.

63

She looked to Billy. "Give me your bag sweet heart. I'll wash everything by hand," she said and extended her hand to Billy.

Billy handed Maria his bag and smiled again. His cheeks were beginning to hurt from so much of it. "Thank you Aunt Maria. For everything," he said with real meaning.

She rubbed his head and watched her son and Billy run out the door and into the field of Tangerine trees just across the road. The screen door slammed behind them. Billy ran behind his cousin Manny, but had no idea where they were going. He ran near the trees and saw the birds scattering as they came close.

"I can't wait for you to see this place!" called Manny to his cousin. "You've got to promise you won't tell anyone else, OK?" he yelled out.

Billy didn't know what he was getting into, but didn't care. It was his first adventure and he was going to enjoy it completely. "I promise!" he called back.

"Especially not my sisters!" Manny quickly added. "They'll ruin it for us," he said and continued to run.

"OK!" Billy said, but wondered why. He didn't have any brothers or sisters, so he didn't know why they shouldn't know.

They came to a clearing about five hundred feet from the house and Manny stopped running. Billy stopped next to him. Breathing heavily. That was the most he'd run in his entire life at one time and was winded.

"You OK?" asked Manny.

"Sure," Billy said in-between breaths.

"Good, my mother will kill me if you get hurt," he said, a little worried.

"I'm fine, don't worry," Billy said, not looking to seem odd in front of his cousin. "Where is this place?" he said with genuine curiosity.

"It's just beyond those trees We're not too far," he said, pointing over a vast field of wild flowers towards a large patch of oak trees draped in Spanish moss.

They took off through the field of wild flowers and were swallowed by them. Manny opened his arms to feel the plants as he ran and Billy followed suit. He was almost overwhelmed by all of the smells at once. The rich floral fragrance took over all other smells until they made it to the woods.

Billy looked up at the majesty of the old oaks and was taken in by their beauty.

"Look where you're going, Billy, you'll run right into a tree," Manny shouted in warning.

Billy looked down, saw another large oak in front of him and dodged it at the last moment. "Thanks!" he shouted back.

"It's just through here," Manny said and slowed to a walk as he led him into a maze made entirely of grapevines. Hundreds upon thousands of red and white grapes hung in bunches from the many branches.

Billy stared in amazement at the beauty of the work of art he was walking through. Whoever had built this had taken a lot of time and effort to keep it so manicured. As they went deeper and deeper into the maze of vines, Billy wondered if they would ever find their way out.

"Don't worry, I know this place like the back of my hand," Manny said, seeing the look on Billy's face.

"OK, good, I was a little worried. Is *this* the secret place?" Billy said.

"Oh, no... This is just the way in," Manny said and led Billy deeper and deeper in until they saw it.

A large perimeter of fruit trees stood beyond a seven foot archway made entirely of blue, white and violet flowers growing from an ancient vine as thick as

Billy's small wrist. The vines grew into the thicket of trees as though nature had intended for these plants to grow together.

At the center of the entangled mesh of fruit trees was a small cottage made of earthen clay and covered entirely by a mosaic pattern of stones. The rocks were placed in waves around the home in a design that forced the viewer into a hypnotic gaze.

Around the small dwelling was an intricate pattern of flower and vegetable beds. Each planted next to each other in a large nexus creating the most beautiful garden he could ever imagine. He looked at his cousin in amazement. "This is *your* secret spot?" he said in amazement.

A large white male cat walked up to Manny and rubbed up against his leg. He reached down to pet him. "Hiya big guy, how are you today?" he asked and scratched him under his chin. The cat just raised his chin for Manny so he could do a proper job of it. He had two different colored eyes; one blue and the other golden-yellow. He cooed to the cat, "You're a good kitty, aren't you?" he looked up to Billy. "No... this isn't *my* place. I just discovered it," he laughed and said with pride.

"Then whose is it?" Billy pleaded.

"This place is *Mr. Caytoe's*," he said with a mysterious flare to his words.

"Who's Mr. Caytoe?"

"Mr. Caytoe is a magician."

"A magician?" Billy asked. "A for *real* magician?"

"Oh... yeah," Manny lowered his voice. "I heard my father talking to my mother about him one night after he came back from the bar with his friends. When my dad's drunk he says amazing things, so I always try to listen. Sometimes he doesn't make a lot of sense, but mostly he's really funny," he giggled.

"What'd he say?"

"Well, from what I remember, Mr. Caytoe was trying to sell some of his vegetables to a local official and they wouldn't take his food because they hadn't inspected his property. Then he asked Mr. Caytoe to show them where he was growing his food, because they didn't even know that he lived in the area. Mr. Caytoe refused to tell them and they tried to have him arrested, but when the local police tried to take him, he just whispered a few words in front of them and waved his hand like this," swirling his fingers in front of him. "The police officer just stood there, looked into space and forgot where he was. The farming official just turned around and walked away. Mr. Caytoe didn't say anything. He just put his vegetables in the back of his truck and drove away," said Manny.

"No way..." Billy said, mystified.

"Yes way... Look at this place," he said and waved his hand quickly. "Who could take care of it all alone, with *no* machinery? Our family has to use machines for everything or we'd have no tangerines to sell," said Manny.

"So, where is he now? Does he know you come here?" Billy said, now worried.

"He goes to the market to sell his crops every day at this time. He shouldn't be back for a while now," not showing fear in front of his cousin.

"Does he let you come here?" asked Billy.

"Not necessarily, but I don't hurt or take anything. I just like to come play with his cats. He has seven of them and they're all really nice. They kind of guard this place for him when he's gone. They're *really* smart cats," he said.

A gray truck pulled into a smooth stoned driveway in front of Mr. Caytoe's place.

"Oh, man, he's home! Let's go!" Manny said, grabbed his cousin's arm and ran away quickly.

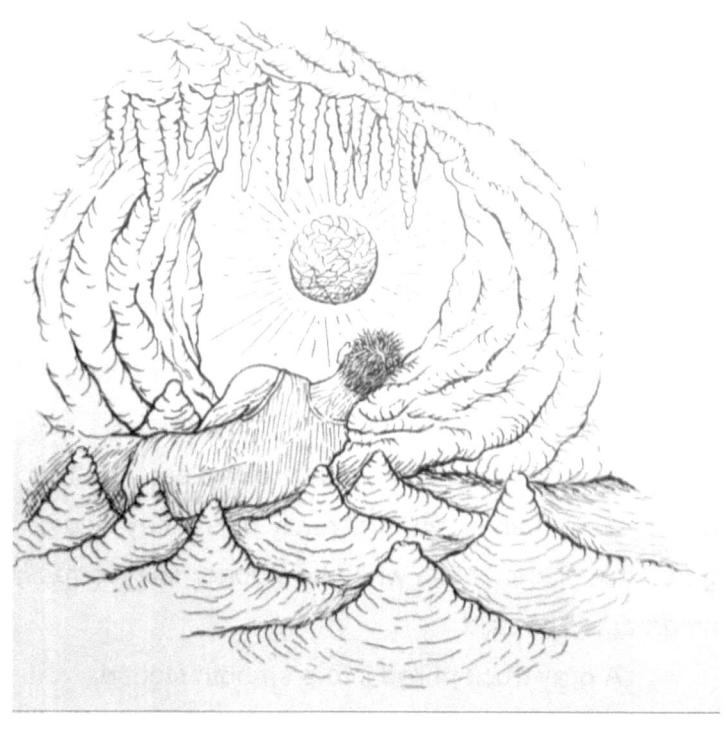

SIX

....

AN UNCOMMON FRIENDSHIP

Takeshi woke to the feel of cold rain on his face. He stirred and tried to push himself up, but felt immediate pain shoot throughout his entire body. His leg throbbed in his right foot and ankle and he couldn't breathe without his ribs wanting to make him scream in anguish.

For a brief moment, he didn't know how he got where he was, but then it all came quickly back to him. Tears streamed down his eyes as he remembered that he told no one where he was going and none of his father's staff would be back from vacation for at least another three days.

For the first time in a while Takeshi longed to see his father. In-between sharp breaths, he tried to think of where his father was right now. His baseball team, the San Francisco Giants had won the World

Series just a few weeks prior and the team, including all senior management was on a world tour celebrating their team's success. He felt an emotion that he didn't think he had, bitterness.

In this one small moment in Takeshi's young life, he forgot about his journey to become the greatest baseball player of all-time and just wanted to be in the comforts of his beautiful home with a loving family. Something he thought he might never do again.

An anger at his own carelessness cascaded through him, making him forget the extraordinary pain he was in. He pulled himself forward in the darkness, not knowing what direction he was going in. His body was on fire, but that didn't matter to him at the moment.

The droplets of icy rain fell harder and Takeshi knew that he needed to find shelter from it. If the weather got any colder, it might turn to hail or frozen rain.

His eyes began to adjust to the darkness and he thought he saw a small cave big enough for him to escape the weather. He dragged his body to it, using his arms to pull forward and his left leg to push him along, each time sending new waves of pain throughout his broken body. Though the cave was only about twenty-five feet from him, it seemed as if it were a mile.

The rain fell faster, completely soaking his already frozen body and suddenly turned to hail the size of a small pebble, but still enough to make him cry out into the night, "Help me, God! I'm not ready to die!" His voice was engulfed by the sound of the hail striking thousands of surrounding trees.

He felt a surge of strength like never before and continued to drag his body to the small opening. He closed his eyes and thought of nothing else but the cave.

The hail grew larger and began to strike him hard. He gritted his teeth and grabbed anything in front of him. His right ankle bumped into a jagged rock underneath him and it felt as if someone had stabbed him in the leg. He ignored the unbelievable pain and continued forward.

Takeshi opened his eyes again and saw the darkness of the cave in front of him. It was only four feet high, but at least eight feet wide. He summoned what was left of his strength and rolled himself into it.

He lay on his back and stared upward. Small stalactites hung from the ceiling, leaving him little space above. Though the hail stopped pelting his body, he now felt like he was in a horizontal iron maiden. His body shivered in the cold. The hail stopped and was replaced by a slightly warmer rain. Takeshi took short breaths, trying to control the pain from his ribs and listened to the sounds of the rain for a long time until he fell to slumber.

It was still dark when he suddenly opened his eyes a few hours later and felt the presence of another in his vicinity. His leg and ribs still pounded from inside-out, but were controlled due to his stillness.

He turned his head to the left and looked up toward the top of the tall crevice in the Earth and saw a shimmering orb float in circles, then lowered slowly toward him. His body froze in fear. He knew there was nothing he could do to stop it and had no choice but to wait. As it guided itself toward him, he looked closely at its structure. Though luminescent, he could still see through it.

For a moment Takeshi thought it was the light given off from a flashlight. "Could someone be looking for me?" he thought. He tried to call out, but all that came out of his throat was a deep gurgling sound. He tried again and could only manage a soft "help" until his throat closed up again.

The orb flew closer to him and hovered at the opening of the cave. His fear turned to curiosity as he did not feel as though it could harm him. His body relaxed and the two stood inspecting each other.

Takeshi could now see that it looked like a bubble. Though glowing, it had what seemed to be mass. Almost as if it contained the entirety of the Universe; a complex system of lights and strings that connected together like an individual cell in the human brain.

A tiny voice spoke his name, but he did not hear it with his ears. "Hello Takeshi it has been a long time my friend," it said.

Takeshi's eyes opened wide and thought, "I must be hallucinating." The bubble did a little dance up and down as it giggled like a small boy.

"You are not hallucinating. I am quite real," he laughed and giggled again. "We have been friends as long as time. You may not remember me now, but in time it will all come back to you," said the bubble.

"Friends? How could we be friends? I have never seen you in my life." He paused for a moment and looked behind it to see if there was someone behind the bubble playing a bad joke. "I must be dreaming," Takeshi said perplexed.

The bubble danced up and down again. "Of course you're dreaming, but that still does not mean that I am not real or that we are not friends. Life is just a *word* created by man to justify his existence. You have always been and will always be alive. How you look while you are doing it changes with the setting of the sun, or so it seems to me at times," said the shimmering bubble. Takeshi momentarily forgot his wounds and breathed in deep, causing him to wince with the sharp pain. The bubble continued, "You have asked to live the life you were meant to lead in your time on this Earth, and as your friend I am here to remind you of this," said the bubble.

Angered at his renewed pain, Takeshi spoke aloud, "How will that help me now? I'm at the bottom of a pit. My ankle and ribs are broken, how can a tiny bubble help me?"

The bubble spoke again to his thoughts, "I am *not* this tiny bubble you see. Like you are not the young man you have seen in the mirror for so many years." Its voice was once again soothing.

Takeshi's body began to vibrate and he felt a wave of energy shoot through him, providing immediate relief to his pain. Takeshi was baffled. "Oh my God, did you do that? The pain is gone," he said and breathed deeply for the first time since his fall.

"Yes, but only to show you that your healing has begun. I cannot fix you; you must fix you. That is why you are here. That is why anyone chooses to live on Earth," it said.

"What do you mean? It doesn't make sense," said Takeshi.

"All will come in time, but for now my purpose is to guide you back to yours," the bubble communicated with sincerity. "You must find your way to the base of the great mountain, you call Mount Shasta. There you will discover your true purpose and reason for being," said the bubble.

"Mount Shasta? How I am I going to get there, let alone get out of this stupid ravine," Takeshi said in frustration.

"You will find a way. You always do," it said and its inside mass of light changed in front of Takeshi's eyes to form a smile. "I'll see you soon my friend, I have to go now," it said and began to drift upward.

"Go? Don't go, please... I need help!" Takeshi called out.

"You've had all the help you need. It's time for me to visit another," it said and continued its path to the cloudy Heavens above.

"What is your name? How can I call you again if I need you?" Takeshi yelled in desperation.

Just as it was about to drift out of the ravine the bubble sent one final thought. "My name is Ishmael," he paused, "It's up to you, Takeshi. It's all up to you." And Ishmael disappeared.

Takeshi yelled out, "No…don't leave me!" He cried silently for a long time until he drifted off again, the whole time thinking about Ishmael.

....

SEVEN

JOURNEY INTO THE MIST

Ru-Ado stormed through the forest as angry as he had ever been. Even though he wanted more for his life besides just surviving, he had always seen himself leading his tribe of zuzuans after his father had gone back into the Earth. His father's last words to him stuck in his mind, "Unless you learn compassion, you will never be the leader you seek to be." They repeated over and over.

He remembered shaming h s uncle, Sho-Ana-Do in front of his father and brother, even though he had no chance at beating Ru-Ado in a fight. It was a shame that sent him off tearing into the woods and called attention to the human hunters.

He grunted loudly and struck a nearby birch tree that had been standing for much longer than Ru-

Ado was brought to the Earth by his mother and father.

The tree fell with a crash onto another smaller white birch, also sending it to its eventual death. "What don't I know about compassion?" he thought as he took a seat on the fallen giant. "I am zuzuan! A warrior of the forest and I cower to no one," he paused. "Do the humans show compassion for the many deer and elk they kill every day, taking food away from our people? Does the bear show compassion for the fish it eats from the river? No, they do not! Only the strongest survive as long as our oldest warriors," he said, answering himself.

His grandfather, the Sho-Han, the tribe's spiritual leader had seen more winters than any zuzuan ever spoken of and before Ru-Ado had reached his massive height and strength, was the deadliest of them all.

The birds began to sing again above him and a light rain started to fall. He lifted his face to it and let it wash over him, enjoying the coolness it brought in the middle of the day.

His stomach rumbled with hunger. It was a pain he tried to ignore for the last day, but now there was no denying it. The few nuts and berries he was able to find were not enough for his massive body.

He smelled deeply, hoping for an easy meal, but the sun was at its highest and there were not many other creatures brave enough to hunt at this time of day. He drew in another huge breath through his nose and caught what he was hoping for. A boar was close by. "I'm too weak to run for too long. If I cannot catch him, maybe I will be able to snatch his fleeing prey," he thought. Zuzuan were not scavengers by choice, but had no problem taking a meal if it presented itself to them.

The boar's scent became stronger and Ru-Ado knew it was coming closer. He also knew that if he was hunting with the tribe, the boar would have no chance to escape, but without their help he would have to trap the boar on his own. A brown hare darted out from under the bushes across from Ru-Ado. Its eyes were feverish as it tried to escape the hungry boar.

Ru-Ado looked at the rabbit with interest, but only that, as it was far too small to even think about eating. It would cost him more energy than it was worth to him. His goal was now the boar. If he could capture it without incident he would have a meal for at least a couple of days, depending on its size. Some boars were known to grow as large as an elk calf and twice as heavy. Ru-Ado waited patiently, trying not to make a sound. He knew he was up-wind, meaning that the boar would not smell his presence ahead of him. The boar barreled through the brush, its large tusks ripping and tearing the fresh vegetation out of its way. He looked from side to side for the hare.

Ru-Ado stood crouched behind a large tree, ready to snatch it up. The boar ran past his tree and Ru-Ado pounced, grabbing the boar by its hind legs. It squealed loudly and tried to wriggle itself free from his tight clutches. Normally Ru-Ado would try to kill his prey quickly by snapping its neck and tried to get his hands around the boar's neck, but it was too thick around. The wily snaggle-haired beast saw that he had a chance for survival and swiped its tusks at Ru-Ado, gashing his leg and opening his thick skin to the air. Ru-Ado roared in pain as blood began to drip down his leg.

He swiped his free hand hard across the boar's neck and heard it snap in two. Now that the boar was no longer a danger he let it drop to the ground and feasted on his first large meal in nearly a week. His ravenous hunger was finally satisfied and made him very sleepy. He found a thick grouping of large trees and lay down to rest in the middle of them. The wet ground never felt so good as he stretched and curled onto his side.

As Ru-Ado waited for slumber he thought about his father and his journey to the Sacred Grounds to bury Sho-Ana-Do. "When I wake I will eat again and bring what I can to Ado-Han," his anger now melted with a full stomach. "He will need my help carrying Sho-Ana-Do." He knew that the journey to the Sacred Grounds was at least three moons away from where they were and no matter how tall and strong Ado-Han was Sho-Ana-Do was not a small zuzuan. He was dead weight and very heavy. Ru-Ado knew Ado-Han couldn't be traveling fast and figured that he could catch up to him before he arrived at the Zuzuan Holy Land. Ru-Ado let sleep come and had a rare peaceful rest.

He woke in the early hours of the next morning to a thick fog and was barely able to see in front of him. Ru-Ado was afraid of nothing, but there was something about the low laying clouds that made him feel uneasy. He stood and felt a sharp pain from the wound the boar gave him and winced. Flies flew to the

85

open wound and knew he would have to clean it out in the water soon.

He gazed panoramically and called out a long low-pitched howl that rose slowly and lasted for nearly a minute; his powerful lungs able to hold an incredible amount of air. The sound traveled through the vastness of the land.

Ru-Ado listened closely for any response, not knowing if there were any other zuzuan tribes in the area. Though an aggressive people, they respected each other's space and would not violate that respect for any reason. There was a code among the zuzuan people that was taught from the time of their birth; each zuzuan to their own.

Ru-Ado howled again, this time twice as long and finished with a flurry of quick, sharp hoots. If there were any other zuzuans on the hunt, they would know there was another in the area that came in peace.

Ru-Ado looked for what remained of his boar and saw it lying where he left it hours before. He was glad for that small piece of comfort, but he also knew that no other animal would dare touch his meal in fear of becoming his next one.

He looked back into the wet and airy thickness around him and saw a figure drifting toward him. Ru-

Ado crept quickly behind a tree and peered at it from a distance.

Whatever it was, it was very tall, almost a foot taller than him. He was stunned to think that there was someone in the forest larger than the zuzuan, but there it was. His curiosity got the better of him as he limped over to the boar, bent down and tossed it over his shoulder; moving quickly towards the large creature. Ru-Ado noticed it wore a shroud over the white hair on its head and dark blue body. Ru-Ado was perplexed, "Is that a human?" he thought. He hadn't heard of any humans to reach such enormous heights, but followed it all the same.

He walked slow and quiet behind the creature for a long time before it stopped and turned, looking directly at Ru-Ado. Its blue face had black lines drawn under its eyes, traveling down the f gure's face and onto its neck, swirling around his thick muscles and disappearing under the cover of its shroud. This was no human and he knew it. It's eyes expressionless as it waved for Ru-Ado to continue following him. It turned around and traveled into the distance. The fog lifting slightly, but still full enough to litter the darkness with its white cover. Ru-Ado felt compelled to follow as this was the strangest moment of his life.

The Sho-Han had once told a tale to his tribe of a giant people from the times long before his great-grandfather's grandfather who were much larger and stronger than the zuzuan. Their skin was as blue as the first flowers that come in spring and like the humans after them, had no hair on their bodies, except for their heads, which were covered in white hair that shined like a spider's web after the rain.

They were a people that ruled the land for thousands of years until the Earth took back dominion in a great flood of water. Some of these people escaped the waters through deep tunnels under the mountain at the edge of the Zuzuan Sacred Grounds.

Ru-Ado did not know if he was one of these ancient people, but knew there was something about him that demanded respect as he walked proud and graceful.

Ru-Ado continued behind him until the sun had risen completely and burned through the dense fog. The hooded figure turned again to him, but this time his face had changed, carrying nothing but an intense glow. Ru-Ado was confused, but couldn't remove his stare from him.

It raised its arm to Ru-Ado and made a friendly gesture with his now glowing hands and vanished right in front of him. Ru-Ado was shocked by the suddenness of his departure, but his amazement turned quickly as he caught the smell of something very familiar; a human.

In the distance, just beyond where the hooded figure had gone, came the sound of a young human crying out in pain. "No.... ah...." as it fell into something; then a rumbling crash onto a pile of fallen branches. A scream followed like none ever to fall upon his ears. It was a cry of pain, anguish and determination. Ru-Ado walked carefully towards the sound not knowing what to expect, especially after what he had just seen.

EIGHT

....

A LESSON LEARNED

Takeshi crawled on the wet ground that barely saw sunlight looking for mushrooms to eat. His father had taken him on a rare trip into the woods to find large Porcini mushrooms and many others to make a famous soup his grandmother had prepared for Hiro many times before she passed on.

Hiro taught his son what was poisonous and what was edible in the forest. "If it is red, then expect to be dead," he would repeat over and over after passing one on the ground.

Takeshi had already managed to eat several grubs he had dug from the ground and a large cricket, but wanted to get the nasty taste out of his mouth. The grubs weren't too bad to him as they had a nutty flavor, but eating the cricket almost made him throw up the tasty bugs.

He dragged his broken body to a fallen tree and found what he was looking for, a large cluster of white and tan Oyster mushrooms. He grabbed a large mushroom from the cluster and began eating it immediately; the taste sending waves of pleasure through his body. "Oh my God, this is good," he said aloud and ate the rest of the mushroom quickly. He grabbed another and ate it as well, but more slowly this time as to enjoy the rest of his meal. He didn't know how long he would have to stay within the ravine and wanted to save the rest of this delicacy for another time.

Since his visit from Ishmael two days before he had less and less pain in his ankle and ribs, but still lacked the strength to attempt climbing to the top of the embankment above him.

He still questioned whether or not his experience with the glowing bubble was a dream or real, but was glad for it. He felt a greater sense of self and protected by the idea that he was not alone.

Takeshi rolled over to see the sky and was rewarded with a bolt of lightning from within his rib cage. Tears ran down the sides of his eyes and into his ears. He turned his head from side to side to remove the fluid from his ears and controlled his breathing. If he didn't expand his lungs too far, the pain was lessened to a dull ache that remained as long as he was motionless.

In times like this Takeshi tried to think of anything, but the pain and sent his thoughts to what Ishmael had said about his calling in life. He knew that Mount Shasta was to the north of him and wondered how long it would take him to get there. "Once I get out of here, I'm not going back home. There is no home for me to go to," he had decided.

Tears welled up in his eyes again when he thought of his father being so far away, but also felt anger toward him for always leaving him alone with strangers who only cared about getting a pay check from the billionaire.

He resented his father's love for his work over his love for him, but also knew that his father didn't know any better. That was his way of life and Takeshi was going to have to learn how to live with it; whether he liked it or not. He caught his tears and held them in. "I'm done crying about this! I'm getting out of here tomorrow," he screamed to the sun. He tightened his face and rolled back over, feeling every inch of the pain, but refusing to acknowledge it. He grimaced his face and crawled back to his cave to get some rest and hoped it would rain again so he could catch enough water to quench his mouth and body. He loathed drinking from the few muddy puddles he found on the ground and wished for clean water.

He lay staring at the rock formations above him and imagined what it would feel like to have his mouth filled with clean delicious water with deep feeling; his want radiated throughout his body.

As if by magic, drops of water began to fall on his face from the stalactite above. The cool droplets of liquid fell on his cheek with increasing rapidity.

Stunned, but thrilled at the same time, Takeshi shifted his body over to line himself up with the falling water, ignoring the pain and opened his mouth wide, catching as much of it as he could. He let it fill his mouth completely and took a deep swallow. Takeshi turned his head quickly so he could take a breath without the water falling into his mouth at the same time. "It's so good," was all he could manage before turning his head back to the water. He drank again and again until his need weakened. He thought, "That's enough for now," and just as quickly as the water began to flow from gray rocks above him, it stopped, but one final droplet of water fell and hit the tip of his nose. Takeshi laughed out loud like a man who had crossed a long and lonely desert. He closed his eyes and gave himself to sleep once again.

Takeshi woke on his third day at the bottom of the ravine feeling different. His once comfortable running sneakers felt tight against his feet and much of the pain in his right ankle had lessened greatly. He tried to move his ankle a bit, just to test it out, but the pain had not gone away completely. He winced from the tenderness still left in the area. He wiggled the toes on his left foot to test how much space they still had and was startled to discover that there was none; his toes pressed against the tip of his sneaker.

Takeshi thought, "Is it possible I've grown overnight?" puzzled by the sudden change. He breathed deep to test the recovery of his broken ribs and was again astonished to feel considerably less pain. He smiled and thought, "Is this possible? How could I be healing so quickly?" ther thought, "It would be wonderful if I could have a drink of water right now." As quickly as the thought entered his mind, water began to flow from the stone above him and landed on his face.

He opened his mouth, took a large gulp of water and swallowed quickly, letting the liquid sooth his body and soul. He drank again and again until his aching stomach was filled. He then thought, "I've had enough for now, I need some food." He smiled again when the water ceased to fall down onto him and rolled to his left and onto his stomach. The pain was there but much less than the day before.

A look of purpose crossed his face as he crawled back to the log that held the few remaining Oyster mushrooms and discovered that the two mushrooms he had eaten previously had been replaced by two new equally sized mushrooms, giving him more than enough food for an entire day. He ate three mushrooms this time, but savored the flavor of them all and chewed his food with care.

After a few minutes of rest he remembered his promise to himself about getting out of the hole in the ground, but knew he couldn't do it on his stomach. He pulled himself up to the log that was home to the Oyster mushrooms, grabbed the log with his right hand and brought up his left knee. The pain in his ribs flared briefly, but allowed him this large task. Takeshi pushed off of his foot and kept his hand firm against the log, sending his body upward and straight for the first time in three days.

He stood at his full height and let the tears of joy run down his cheek.

"Thank you, Ishmael," he said quietly with his eyes closed. He felt an enormous wave of love rush through him from the tip of his toes to the standing blades of black hair on his head. He opened his eyes and looked around him. He saw how much smaller his cave was from a standing position. He turned his eyes skyward and looked at the top of the ridge and noticed it was an almost vertical ascension from every earthen wall.

Takeshi lowered his chin to his chest and closed his eyes. He slowed his breath and tried to think of a way out without re-injuring himself too badly, but knew there was no easy way to co it. He opened his eyes. "I'm going to Mount Shasta and there isn't a thing on this Earth that can stop me,' he said to the wind swirling around him. He took his first step to freedom and felt another lightning bolt zoom through his body. He ignored the pain again and kept his mind focused on reaching the top of the dirt wall in front of him. One foot after another, he limped heavily until he had no more room to walk but up. He let his body fall forward slowly and used his arms to brace for impact.

Above him was a large root jutting out of the ground. He reached out to it and pulled himself upward and pushed up with his good leg, focusing on

97

his breath and reached out for another within his grasp.

Within an hour Takeshi had almost reached the top. All that was left for him to climb was a small lip that jutted out slightly from the rest of the embankment. A large rough rock stuck out of the lip and provided what Takeshi thought was his final step to freedom.

Takeshi laughed to himself. "This wasn't that hard at all. It took me longer to learn how to hit a curve ball," he said and shook his head in disbelief. He grabbed for the stone, but the rock slipped right out of the ground and sailed over his head and onto the ground below. Takeshi lost his balance and slid all the way back down the steep hill and onto a pile of fallen branches.

He screamed like never before as pain shot through his entire body. "I am not going to die in here!" he called into the wind. "If it takes me a thousand times and a hundred broken bones, I *am* getting out of here!" he screamed.

Then he heard them; slow but heavy steps walking in his direction. His determination and resolve melted with the fear of the unknown. Every impulse in him wanted to scream for help, but knew that no human could make such a loud noise just stepping through the forest. He thought, "What the heck is that?" and looked for a place to hide. Before he could move a muscle, it peered over the narrowest part of the ravine and stared straight at him.

"Oh my God," was all he could manage as the albino Sasquatch let out a horrendous roar so loud that he felt its vibration.

Then something incredible happened within him, his fear evaporated and was replaced by an intense feeling of rebellion. Without knowing why or where it came from, Takeshi roared back at the beast as loud as he could, his voice cracking when he ran out of breath. "I'm not afraid of you! If you want me, you're going to have to come down here and get me!" he shouted at the creature.

The Sasquatch roared back at him, this time even louder than before and knocked back Takeshi on the ground with its force. He was furious at the courage of the human, but was curious all the same. The Sasquatch picked up a rock the size of a soft ball and threw it directly at Takeshi, which barely missed his head by a few feet. The boulder was thrown with such force that it stuck right into the wet ground.

Takeshi looked back at the stone and became even more enraged at the beast. He mustered all the strength he could and stood tall below him, feeling no pain. "You throw like a girl, you ugly bastard!" he screamed. He bent down to the ground, picked up a stone the size of a baseball and threw it directly at the Sasquatch, but it fell short as his strength was at a minimum. The pain in his ribs tore through his torso and back, but he still stared at the animal as if he was the one who was looking for a fight.

The Sasquatch grunted at him with a series of clicks, hoots and low howls and to Takeshi's ears some of what he said sounded vaguely familiar to his father's native language. He looked at the beast anew and tried a new tactic, yelling in Japanese, "Either you help me or you're going to have to come down to kill me, but I'm not afraid of you." He saw that the creature turned his ear to him to listen more closely, as if he understood what he said.

Takeshi yelled again, "Go on! Get out of here, if you're not going to kill me, then let me die alone!" He turned his back to the creature and walked slowly back to his cave. He waited for the Sasquatch to respond, expecting another stone to be hurled at him, but it never came. He made it to the cave and crawled

100

in on his hands and knees. Every inch of him wanted to look back at the creature, but he knew that would show a sign of weakness.

He heard the creature walk around the small valley and then the noise of a tree being pushed down the side of the ravine. Takeshi turned to see if the Sasquatch was going to use the tree to climb down and kill him, but he only heard the softening thuds of it walking away.

Takeshi waited a long time before leaving his cave again that day, just in case the creature was waiting for him to show himself. He still felt the effects of adrenaline when he realized that the animal had provided his bridge to freedom.

He waited a few more hours for darkness; drank heavily from the stalactite and ate the remaining Oyster mushrooms and walked to the fallen tree.

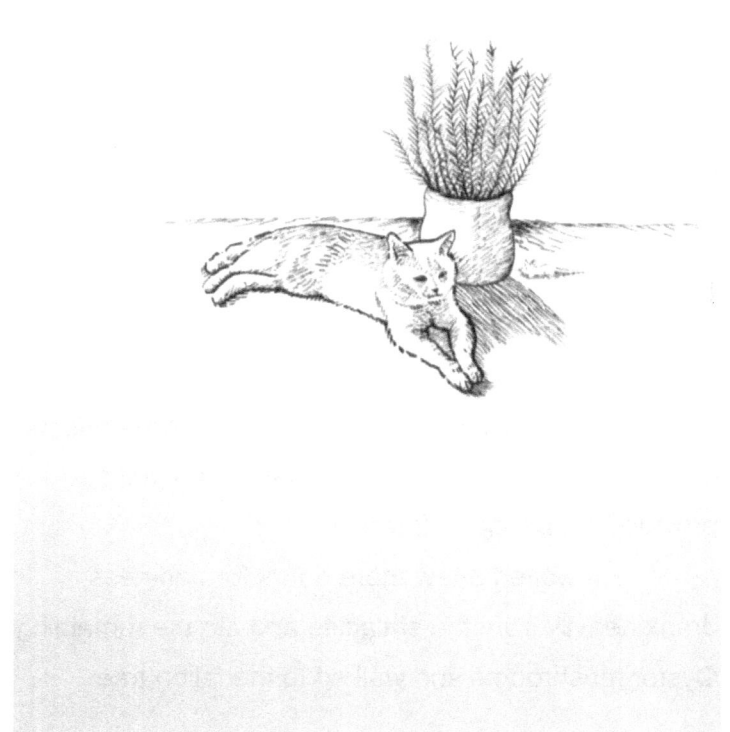

NINE

....

MR. CAYTOE

Mr. Caytoe stepped out of his old gray pick-up truck and closed the door behind him. He was six feet tall, slender and very tan. He wore blue jeans and a black t-shirt. His long wavy hair and trimmed beard were salt and pepper gray. He had light green eyes and an easy way about him. He walked with his shoulders straight and confident to the back gate of his truck, pulled the handle and guided it down gently. He reached in and grabbed the first of four wooden boxes containing the fruits and vegetables he was unable to sell or trade.

There were lemons, limes, oranges, tangerines and grapefruits stacked high in three of the boxes. The last held a variety of fresh herbs that were wrapped in wet towels to keep them healthy during transport from his property to the local farmer's market.

As he carried the last of the boxes to his cold storage shed his best friend and guard-cat, Hathor, greeted him.

"Hi, Caytoe!" said the large white male cat. His mew was high-pitched and lengthy.

"Hiya, Hathor ole' buddy. Holding up the fort?" Caytoe said in return.

"Of course," Hathor purred.

"Good, good. Anything happen while I was gone?" said Caytoe.

"Yes," Hathor meowed in a long drawn out manner.

"Really? Was it anyone I know?" Caytoe asked.

"Two boys," said Hathor.

"Hmm... The boys I've been expecting?"

"Yes," Hathor meowed in the affirmative.

"Good. I'm glad the boy Manny brought his cousin over so soon. How did he look?" Caytoe asked.

"Not so good," Hathor purred.

"Sad, huh? No doubt. He's been through a lot," Caytoe said and looked around his property. "Has everyone eaten today?" he asked of the six other cats that roamed the property and lived outside of his home.

"Yes," meowed Hathor.

"Good, they've taken care of our mouse problem then, huh?"

"For now."

"Excellent. Listen ole' pal, I've got some work to do for our new friend. Do you think you can manage without me for a few days?" Caytoe asked.

"Are you kidding, you're always someplace else," Hathor said as if he were offended.

"Perfect. I've got to see if I can find his parents," said Caytoe, ignoring Hathor's sarcasm.

"They're alive?"

"Oh, they're alive," Caytoe said and smiled big.

"How?" asked Hathor.

"I'll explain later. For now I just need you to make sure no one interrupts my work. I'll need complete focus for this journey," Caytoe said, very serious.

"No problem," Hathor assured.

"Thanks, Hathor," Caytoe said and bent down to give his friend a good long scratch on his head and neck. "When I get back, I'm gonna have to comb that hair of yours bud, you're starting to molt," Caytoe said as he pulled loose white hair off of his hands.

"Meow..." Hathor complained.

"I know, I know, I've promised before, but I really really promise this time."

"We'll see," Hathor said and gave him a crooked stare.

Caytoe laughed out loud and rubbed him on his head once again before walking to his garden behind the ornately decorated earthen home. He inspected each of his flower and vegetable beds and picked any dead leaves from the plants, feeling the soil in each to make sure they had enough moisture.

Caytoe looked to the sky and saw that the clouds were grayish-white, scattered and low and knew that it would rain soon, giving the plants the needed water while he was gone.

Caytoe picked a few stems from the rosemary, oregano, basil, dill and parsley plants and ate them on the spot. Chewing carefully for a full minute before swallowing deeply. "Mm... that's good," he said in delight.

He walked over to a wooden barrel and removed the cover to reveal a clear pool of water. He reached down for a cup that was attached to a chain on the barrel and scooped it into the water. He whispered a few words to the cup and drank the clear liquid. "Ah..." he sighed and repeated the process twice more. He replaced the cover on the barrel and walked to his perimeter of interconnected fruit trees and saw that they were growing a bit out of line. He walked up to an old lemon tree. "You seem to be growing a bit haggard, my friend. Do you think it possible if you could bring your branches in line with the others?" he whispered. With his words the lemon tree's overgrown branches immediately began to weave themselves into the others, only a few seconds passing before they looked perfectly manicured.

"Thank you, you are looking beautiful these days. Your lemons are delicious and keep me healthy," Caytoe said and watched the tree's leaves wiggle about as though a light breeze passed through them. He smiled and walked from tree to tree, assuring they were all perfectly manicured. Caytoe walked away with a large ripe orange in hand, headed to his labyrinth and navigated a path to its center where there was nothing but another wall of grapes ripening on thick vines. "Good afternoon, my friend, you are looking gorgeous these days. When do you think your fruits will be ready to harvest?" Caytoe asked with a smile. The vines wigg ed about, making the grapes bounce up and down. "A week, huh? That's just wonderful. I can't wait to taste them. Do you think

107

you could do me a favor and let me in? I have some work to do for the next few days and need a lot of privacy," he asked.

Without another word the vines began to twist and turn until they opened a path just large enough for Caytoe to walk through. As soon as he crossed the threshold the vines once again wove themselves back into a wall.

"Thank you," Caytoe said as he entered.

The vines wiggled a quick, "You're welcome," and became still once again.

Inside his hidden enclosure was another earthen home, but only as large as a small shed. There were two windows, each on opposite sides, creating plenty of cross ventilation. The shed's wooden door was small and circular.

Caytoe stood in front of the shed and closed his eyes, saying a long silent prayer. He opened his eyes and put his hands together in front of him before pushing them outward and separating them wide. He brought his hands together again and pushed upward. He turned in each direction and repeated the process, finishing with a final push towards the ground and kept his head bowed in prayer for a long time. He walked

into his hardened clay shed and closed the door
behind him.

TEN

....

TEM

The sky glowed pink-blue or a perfect evening in Bubble Valley. White and gray clouds were perfectly placed in front of a high-hanging go den sun. Its soft luminescence provided warmth and energy to all below.

A group of tiny glowing bubbles littered the sky as would a school of fish in the sea, hungry for adventure as they danced and weaved through the air; swirling, climbing and dropping a thousand feet toward the green ground below without a moment's notice. They all moved perfectly synchronous and anticipated each other as seamlessly as if driven by a single thought.

A Pterodactyl zoomed through the air from a much greater height, slicing through the group without worry or care for their concern. The bubbles instantly

111

adapted to the path of the giant bird, creating a circular tube for it to travel. They continued on, turning in a corkscrew motion, parallel to the ground burgeoning with life and color.

Vast blue lakes reflected the sun's rays back to the taller vegetation. Its constantly changing optical illusion drew you in and held your gaze.

The bubbles flew at near sonic speed towards massive trees below, each no less than a mile high, with mighty trunks, fifty feet in width; each leaf the size of an elephant's ear. They raced just above, free and without care towards a massive pyramid city. It was three miles high and four miles wide.

The pyramid was flat on the top and held a single castle-like stone dwelling, fit for a giant king. A wide road spiraled its way down the stone city, creating a means of travel throughout. Smaller homes were constructed directly off of the roads, each with a large vegetable garden in front.

Hundreds of giant humanoid people of all colors were scattered all over the city, busy in a variety of evening tasks. Soft symphonic music of instruments unknown kept the scene peaceful until the bubbles flashed over their heads, making the citizens of the city enjoying a cool evening after dinner duck down low to the ground and shake their fists at the fleeing pack. The serenity was broken.

One of the women walking in her garden conspired with her closest neighbor. She was no less than nine-feet tall, her skin as blue as the finest lapis lazuli stone and eyes as dark as coal. She wore a simple white robe that fell to her reptile skin sandals. Her glowing blonde hair curled down to her thin shoulders. "Those first souls get crazier and crazier every group. When are we going to bring this up to the Mothertree Counsel? They have an entire valley to explore. Why do they have to fly over the city?" Her voice was high and sharp.

"That's if you can even get the chance to see the Counsel these days," said her neighbor who was slightly shorter and heavier than her friend, but otherwise looked very much like her except that she had bright orange hair that had loose curls that reached down to the top of her huge chest. She carried a wide basket of harvested roots similar to a carrot, but violet in color. "It seems to me that the Counsel would be more careful how they treat their fellow citizens," she continued in a huff, "considering that they're about to become citizens, like *us* once again."

"That's if they lose the coming games," the thin woman chimed in, "and they don't think they're going to lose. They're just lucky enough to have the best warrior and gamesmen the valley has ever seen. I don't like anyone telling me what to do more than anyone else, but they did take the Counsel fairly," she said. Her look changed to take on a dreamy quality.

"It seems to me that you have a crush on the mighty Tem," said the plump woman.

"A crush?" the blond woman blushed. "Are you a fool? I'm married, as you very well know. I love my husband." She looked around to see if any of her other neighbors were outside and listening to them talk.

"Alright, alright... I didn't mean to accuse you," said the woman with orange hair.

The blond woman was clearly relieved, "Thank you for your apology, but..." she cooed. "He is very handsome and taller and stronger than any other warrior in Bubble Valley. What woman wouldn't wonder," she said and both women laughed at one another.

High above, the bubbles continued to swirl in a tightly knit group higher and higher into the darkening sky to the top of the valley's mountain peaks, fifty thousand feet from the ground. They circled the valley below, saying good night to the people.

The great mountains surrounding the beautiful land rumbled softly, causing the bubbles to stop their games. In a flash they each found their own home below, as they were each assigned to the many citizens of Bubble Valley.

One of the bubbles darted into the top window of the Counsel's home at the top of the pyramid. It flew through the open window into Tem's bedroom and under his bed. His room was the size of a football field with two, ten-foot open stone windows providing all the fresh air any giant warrior might need. A crash came to his bedroom door, which was the size of a banquet table and made the entire room shake. The tiny bubble quivered even more, thinking that there was another earthquake. The crash came again, but twice as hard as before, this time sending the door wide open. It slammed against the wall and rattled loudly, knocking it off of its hinges.

A fifteen-foot giant man blasted into the room. He had long straight jet-black hair that was tied with a golden string behind his head in a great ponytail. The many folds of his gold and purple robes sailed behind him as a strong wind blew into his room. He had extraordinary violet colored eyes that changed with the lighting of the room. His skin was a deep bronze, showing that he spent a good deal of time outdoors.

Though massive in stature, he had no abnormalities about him. Every woman wanted him and every man wanted to be him. As champion of the Bubble Valley games twenty-five years running and Head Sentinel to the Mothertree, Tem had everything a man in Bubble Valley could want, but he was seething with anger.

"Grandfather is insane! What is he thinking? Nine hundred and twenty-three is not the age to journey alone through the jungles to counsel with the Mothertree," he roared.

A tiny yellow bird flew in through the crippled wooden door and onto Tem's broad shoulder. Chica was Tem's long-time friend and the only living creature he truly gave his ear to since saving Tem's life a long time ago. He had a plume of red feathers shooting out of the top of his head that bounced up and down as he tried to steady himself. "I'm sorry, Tem, but you have no right to be angry at your grandfather's actions. He is still is the Anak Tribe's Chief Counselor to the Mothertree. If she summons him, then there's nothing he can do. It is his duty," the bird chirped.

Tem bellowed, "Is it his duty to get eaten by a roaming pack of feral zuzuan? Or you're just talking foolishness," he countered.

The bird tweeted as it flew up to face his friend. "That was only a silly rumor started by one of the other four tribes. They are just trying to cause fear among the people and more work for your family. For twenty-five years you have made their strongest gamesmen look like children in a playground. They are just trying to distract you from the upcoming games. They figure that if you are off in the jungle every day looking for these savage zuzuans then you will have no opportunity to train," he said.

Tem's attitude changed and puffed out his chest just a little. He chuckled lightly, but became stern once again. "That might be true, but that still doesn't change the facts. He should have at least asked me to travel with him. *I too* am on the Counsel to the Mothertree and know the path well," he said to his friend.

"Ah, so that's what this is about," Chica whistled a knowing tune.

"What do you mean?" Tem asked.

"I think you're jealous of your grandfather?"

"Jealous? I am not, how could you say that?"

"Well, I just think that you had hoped the Mothertree would have asked you to go."

"I... Uh..." Tem raised his meaty hand. "I..." he stopped when cut-off by Chica.

"Come on, Tem, admit it. I know you better than anyone."

"Yeah, well, you wouldn't if you *ever* left me alone." He looked annoyed.

Chica chirped a merry tune to Tem, "You *are* funny sometimes." He flew over to a window and perched. Tem followed him in and sat on his bed. His heavy weight caused his straw mattress to lay low to the ground, almost flattening the tiny bubble hiding underneath.

"Do you think it has to do with the Earth shakes over the last few days?" he asked his little friend.

"Of course it has to do with the Earth shakes. The valley hasn't shaken in thousands of years. Ever since..." The bird drifted off and looked out of the window and over the immense jungle.

"Nas-Tak was entombed by the Mothertree," Tem finished his words.

"Yes, Nas-Tak," Chica agreed.

"You don't think?" Tem asked and took on a very worried look.

This time Chica finished Tem's words. "That Nas-Tak is after the Seed of Hades?" The bird flew up and out of the window, not wanting to be in the room if Tem got angry again. "Yes," he said fluttering high above the land.

"What? Do you know what that means?" Tem boomed out, the force of his voice sending Chica even further outside the window.

"Not directly at least. There is a chance that he is working with one of the other tribes, but this is all speculation. We have no idea what the Mothertree wants from Ishmael," said Chica.

"That's right, it's all up to wonder, but..." he trailed off. "Not if we go on our own little expedition, right?" Tem said.

Chica caught on. "You *are* the Mothertree's Head Sentinel," he paused. "At least for another few months," he said and waited for his friend to respond.

Tem looked startled at his friend's question. "Do *you* think that I'm not going to win the games this year as well? What are you not telling me?" asked Tem.

"Take it easy, Tem," The bird murmured. "I'm not saying anything like it. I'm just stating a fact. The games will be here very soon and I haven't seen you train once. I *am* your Chief Counselor, am I not? And I see the greatest champion in Bubble Valley more concerned about his grandfather's duty than focusing on retaining power for the Anak Tribe. Without passion the games can become a chore Tem and not everyone is fond of chores," he said with deep knowing.

Tem allowed his friend to speak, but didn't agree with him. "Have you seen my competition this year?" he asked.

"Yes, but that doesn't mean anything."

"We won't know whose competing until that morning. Anything can happen. I just say that it might be good if you forgot about chasing down Ishmael. He may be ancient, but he is still healthy and has navigated the jungles for eight hundred years more than you've walked Bubble Valley. I don't think you give him enough credit. He was a great warrior for the Mothertree," said Chica.

"*Was* a great warrior, Chica! Sure, he's healthy enough, but these are mad times. I am concerned for his safety," Tem said, stood up and the bird flew to stay level with his eyes. "I believe that Nas-Tak is making a move through the zuzuans and I am going to assist him in his travels. *I too* have questions for the

120

Mothertree and I don't need to wait until I am called on," he said with decisiveness.

Chica saw the seriousness in his friend's eyes and knew there was no more challenging him. Tem was resolved to action. "When do you plan to go?" Chica asked.

"Tonight, when the moon is at its highest. Are you coming?"

Chica hesitated only for a moment. "Of course. You wouldn't know what to do without me," he chirped.

Tem smiled slyly. "Come with me to dinner, I want to plan this out well." Tem said and walked back out of the room with Chica following close behind.

The tiny bubble drifted out from under Tem's bed, saw that the room was once again empty and zoomed out of the window.

ELEVEN

....

CAYTOE SLIPS TIME

Mr. Caytoe stepped from the hollow of an ancient tree, felled after many thousands of years standing tall in Tipereth, the home of the Mothertree. From out of thin air he stepped on the heavy moss surrounding the fallen giant.

Every inch of him knew that this is where he would find Billy's parents, but didn't know who or where they were. He knew them in Billy's world as children, but hadn't seen them in a very long time. He knew that in this dimension, they could be anyone, but also knew that he would not be in this single place in time unless it was important to his mission.

When he stepped into his small clay shed earlier that day, he only asked to heal the heart of a soul who would be of greatest importance to human-kind. A needed leader for a weak people with more questions than resolve and he knew that Billy was that boy. He knew this task was the culmination of many others before it and trusted that he was ready for the job.

Caytoe escaped to his father's family estate from Montgomery, New York, on the outskirts of the Catskill Mountains just before the nuclear war. He was an independent contractor, but always working so it seemed as if he worked for only one employer.

Caytoe was a master of anything he chose to do, but he enjoyed creating the most. The job that presented itself as the biggest puzzle became his obsession until it was complete and exactly what his client had in mind. It was as if he could read their thoughts without them having to say a word, which meant that he was a very popular man to hire.

Just before the bombs fell, Caytoe did the unthinkable; he stopped working on a job before it was finished for the first time in his life. He didn't bother to contact his client to tell him that he had quit working on his project, nor did he tell anyone he saw on a day-to-day basis; he just left.

He knew he needed to go to his father's home in Florida. It was a place that he never wanted to return to, but knew that he must. Though everyone in his family had died long ago, he decided that he would camp out there until he knew more. Caytoe always listened to his intuition, even if it meant that he would have to let Rome burn behind him. He arrived in the only place he'd call home for the next twenty years, two days before the first of the bombs put a stop to time.

Caytoe stood a tiny creature in a giant world, but feared nothing. He was only a witness to this world. His body was safe and sound in sticky-hot Tangerine Park, Florida.

He smelled deeply and caught the most intoxicating scent he'd ever experienced. "Is that strawberries or lavender and cherries?" he questioned aloud in wonder, turned his head upward and saw why he was in this place.

Just behind the remains of the hollowed-out tree stood a pinecone statue twenty feet high. It was carved and polished out of rose colored marble and was covered completely with swirling green vines sprouting large purple flowers with long yellow pistons.

Though he was not of this world, Caytoe breathed deeply and felt himself wanting to move forward to touch the flowers; to smell and learn the secret of the incredible aroma.

He moved a bit closer and his stomach started to knot-up. He calmed his desire and backed off to where he stood before within the cover of the tree. He heard the thumping of enormous feet in the deep jungle and felt the vibrations run through his soul. A man standing twelve feet high separated two smaller trees in front of the statue and stood in awe at its beauty.

He apparently knew something about the qualities the enticing flowers presented as he tried not to breathe deeply. He took one step back, but still caught the flowers lure. He took one step forward and brought a hairy hand up to a long orange beard, spotted handsomely with silver. His deep-set milky blue eyes squinted at the sunlight directly above the statue. He wore a dinosaur skin tunic and carried a huge metal ax as his only weapon. His sandals were made of leather, but to an animal unknown to Caytoe.

The wizened man was weary of this plant, but felt compelled to move forward. Though he had lived for the last nine hundred and twenty-three years there were still many secrets that had not been revealed to him in this forest. The land that surrounded the Mothertree was still virgin in many aspects. Only the truest champions with the deepest respect for the land were allowed to step on its soil.

Like his grandson, Tem, Ishmael had once been the champion of the Bubble Valley games and Head Sentinel for the Mothertree; the first tree in creation and the wisest soul on the planet. Only three sentinels were chosen each year from the five major tribes and their job was to protect the noble tree.

Though two hundred feet wide and a mile high, the Mothertree was only known to have dropped twelve seeds in its millions of years within the hollows of Earth.

These were not seeds that could just be planted into the ground and watered to produce another tree of the same species. They were seeds for the people of the world to use as they saw fit to change their existence for the better. These skilled warriors were needed to protect the seeds from those who see destruction as their form of creation and pleasure. Only the longest living sentinels knew the location of the seeds and protected them at all costs. Ishmael was the oldest man in Bubble Valley and the surrounding lands and knew a secret that the rest of the world had not. There was a thirteenth seed

127

dropped by the Mothertree and buried far away from its creator.

This seed was meant to be planted only if all other means for positive creation was no longer available to the people. Only then would they have the ability to end everything in creation on Earth and begin anew, with the one who planted the seed as god of the land; it was this seed that was buried beneath Ismael's feet.

He thought back on his long life and many experiences in Bubble Valley with happiness and pride in knowing that he never intentionally harmed another person in the land unless he was attacked first.

Ishmael was grateful for everything and was ready to die for his cause. The seed beneath him needed to be moved to another location. It had been whispered among the people that Nas-Tak had influenced some of the Zuzuan Tribe to cause havoc in order to disguise their true intention; travel to the lands of Tipereth, where they have been banned from entering since the time of the flood on Earth.

Ishmael's grandfather, Anak had led his people underground, unlike his brother, Noah who was tasked to build a ship and survive the aftermath of the Seed of Poseidon. The Seed of Poseidon was supposedly the last seed of the Mothertree's and was planted by a fierce zuzuan leader that became possessed by his need for power. This zuzuans name was Nas-Tak.

The Mothertree could not intercede in Nas-Tak's actions, but it was able to call judgment by embedding him at the center of Mount Sin. Mount Sin was located on the outer edge of Bubble Valley; the same mountain that shook the city of giant people. Ishmael knew this information as true because he had seen it in his dreams. He had even left his body to call on the help of a friend, long lost to life above ground.

Ishmael bent down and scraped the base of the statue with his ax, clearing the vines from the area he wanted to dig. The plant's vines where strong, but not strong enough for his hardened steel ax as he cut through them in a few minutes. He lowered his old body slowly, set his knees upon the ground and moved some dirt away from the base of the statue. He waited for something to happen, but nothing did. He scooped some more and nothing happened again. Ishmael felt more at ease and set out digging his hole as deep as he needed until he found the box the Seed of Hades was held in.

Caytoe watched the old giant bend down to the ground and dig with his hands. He was mindful of the care he took in his work and knew that the giant had validated his weary thoughts about the vines.

What the red haired man didn't know was that the vines began to move in the direction of his neck. His hair had fallen off his shoulders as he bent over, leaving a small spot of bare skin at the nape of his leathery neck. The vine crept slowly, but surely until it almost rested its leaves on the giant old man's skin.

In a flash the man reached behind him and grabbed one of the purple-pedaled flowers, crushing it in his hand and knew immediately that his moment of death had come. He fell on his back and was dead before he hit the ground.

Caytoe sat with his mouth open wide in amazement and waited.

TWELVE

....

A NEW LOOK ON LIFE

Billy and Manny ran up to the last line of tangerine trees before the small clearing that lead to the back of his home and breathed heavily in place for a long time.

"That place is amazing!" Billy finally managed in-between breaths.

"I knew you'd love it," Manny said with pride.

"You go there every day?" asked Billy.

"Just about," he hesitated. "My mom and dad have been fighting a lot lately cause' my dad's been drinking so much," Manny said.

"I thought you said your dad gets funny?"

"Yeah, well, he used to. Now he just gets angry."

"Why?" Billy asked, truly curious. He had never seen his parents drink alcohol and didn't know what it did to people.

"Grandfather has told my parents that he wants us to get out of his house," Manny said and turned his eyes to the ground.

"Why?" Billy asked.

Manny stayed silent long enough that Billy began to feel a little sick in his stomach. "It's because of me, isn't it?" he finally said.

"Yes," Manny said, finally meeting his cousin's eyes.

Billy felt a whole new feeling well up in his throat and wanted to cry, but held it in. "Why does he hate me so much?" he asked.

"My mother thinks it's because you make him remember," Manny said, still somber.

"Remember what?"

"Everything. Our uncle Manny, your mother, your father, your grandfather."

"My grandfather?" Billy perked up.

"Yes, your father's father owned the orchard down the road before he died a few years ago. Don Eduardo and your grandfather Augustin were *not* friends. Don Eduardo has tried to buy his land ever since he died. The lawyers said that the land belonged to someone else, but they couldn't say until a later day."

"No one knows who owns it?" Billy asked.

"No and they probably never will. Don Eduardo has made a lot of enemies in town and not many people are willing to help him."

Billy took in all of this information with a heavy heart. It seemed to him that he had no place on Earth he could call home without feeling stressed. He missed his parents more than ever as the tears began to well up again.

Manny saw his cousin breaking and quickly chimed in, "But my mother has told Don Eduardo that he'll have to get the local authorities to come and take us out of the house. She thinks grandfather is bluffing and is calling it," he said with rebellion in his voice.

"What does that mean?" Billy asked.

"That means that she thinks he's just trying to scare us some more. My father said that he's worse than the church."

"What does the church have to do with it?"

"I don't know, Billy. Adults always confuse me with all their words."

Billy laughed at his cousin because he knew it was true. Manny joined in and they laughed their fear away.

Still smiling, Manny said, "Come on Billy, my mom's making enchilada's tonight. You don't want to eat them cold," as he made a weird face.

"Why?" Billy asked while running behind Manny.

"Because they're *nasty*," he laughed again and ran up to the door and opened it in one motion. "Mom, we're home!" Manny called into the kitchen. Billy followed quickly behind him. They were sweaty, but happy.

Maria walked quickly in the dining room, saw the look on the boy's faces and knew that they were already best friends. She remembered her sister Connie and fought back a tear. "Look at you two! So happy! I love it." She walked over to her son Manny and kissed him on the head. "What a good boy," she said with pride.

"Mom..." Manny said and pulled away from her.

Maria laughed and said nothing. She walked over to Billy, kissed him on the head as well and gave him a big hug, but Billy didn't squirm, he loved his aunt and wanted to show her.

Later that evening the family sat in the living room together, as was their custom. Maria sat in her chair, next to her husband Carlos and read a book. It was "To Kill a Mockingbird" by Harper Lee. She rocked back and forth on the chair's springs and held her lips tight, her eyes fixed on the words.

Carlos was sunk low in his chair and drank frequently from a clear bottle filled with amber liquid. He kept one hand behind his head and the other draped over the side of the chair, swinging his bottle back and forth as he watched the World Series of Baseball on television. He didn't look interested in the game at all. He just kept drinking throughout the night, getting drunker and drunker until he started yelling at the players on the screen.

"How could you miss that ball? It was a meatball. Right in front of the plate." he yelled. The pitcher on the television threw a curve ball on the outside corner. The batter swung and missed again. "Oh my God! Do you see this loco over here? Look at him, he makes millions of dollars playing a child's game and looks like a fool in front of the world," he said as he drank the bottle dry. He held it over his mouth and let the last drops fall. When the bottle was empty he let it fall to the ground without care.

"Look at me," he continued, his words slurring as they came out. "I'm almost homeless, with no job and..." he looked around the house. "...no more whiskey," he said and sunk back into the chair.

Maria ignored her husband's words as if she had seen the same actions from him for years. She got up silently, placed her book down on a small table next to her chair and picked up her husband's bottle. She brought it to the family's breezeway and returned to the living room. She picked up her book, sat down and continued reading as if nothing happened.

Billy sat next to Manny on an oval rug on the floor. The family's orange and white cat lay next to Manny. His tail twitched from side to side as Manny absentmindedly pet his coat of hair.

Manny loved baseball, but never had time to play. From a very young age Manny had learned to take responsibility into his own hands and worked in place of his father in the orchards. He dreamed of playing on a little league team with other children and pitching a no-hitter in front of his entire family. He smiled at the screen and dreamed.

Billy leaned over to Manny, "I'm gonna go to bed. I'm real tired," he whispered in his ear.

Maria overheard her nephew "Goodnight, Billy. Sleep well, my little bird," she said in a sweet voice.

"My mom said that to me every night before I went to bed," Billy said with a smile.

Maria smiled too. "It doesn't surprise me. Our mother said it to us every night when we were children," she said as her eyes became glassy.

"Good night, Aunt Maria. Thank you for everything."

"You're welcome, Billy. Think nothing of it."

"OK. Night, Manny, Uncle Carlos." Manny just nodded to him and Carlos grunted as Billy walked upstairs to Manny's bedroom.

Once under his bed sheets, he curled to his side and brought his pillow in tight. He breathed deep and let sleep come naturally. Like the night before, his body began to vibrate. He still felt fear, but remembered what happened when he calmed his breathing. After a few moments his body became tranquil and let the energy travel through him freely. He let himself bask in the warmth and love it brought to him.

He lifted easily out of his skin and into the air over his bed and watched himself sleeping below. He thought, "This is too cool. I feel so free. I wonder what they look like down stairs?" and without blinking his eyes, he found himself downstairs and hovering over his family.

Uncle Carlos was asleep in his chair. Heavy snores filled the room. Manny sat on his stomach in front of the television so he could hear the game over his father's noises and Aunt Maria remained focused on her book. A tear fell silently down her cheek with only a few pages remaining.

Billy looked around the room and saw that the color of the rug under Manny was a little different and the walls looked light blue instead of chalky white. He thought, "I wonder where my parents are? Are they in heaven or..." without pause his soul zoomed off into the void, swirling round and round as he watched glowing orbs dance all around him, as if protecting him from something. Only a few seconds passed before his tunnel evaporated around him, leaving him covered in the soft glow of a large full moon. He hovered high above a pyramid city and saw a light coming from the castle at the top of the pyramid. Billy's fear was gone and replaced by intense curiosity.

He glided through the air quickly to the light and hovered outside the window to take a look inside.

He was astonished to see two giant versions of his parents, talking to each other on huge chairs in the middle of their vast library. They were dressed in purple robes with gold trimming. Everything about their looks was exactly the same as he remembered them, but they were just much, much bigger.

"Mom! Dad! I'm here! It's Billy!" he called out, but they didn't hear a word he said. They just continued to talk to each other.

"What do you mean that Tem has gone to find Ishmael?" The large woman with long dark hair said in anger to her husband.

His father coughed into his hand. He was long and lanky, with graying black hair. "I mean that he's gone off to find Ishmael. I don't know how better to explain it to you? That's all I know! Just as much as you, but we are not going to help him by debating it. Sometimes I think you just love to argue with me for the sake of having something to do,' he said.

"Oh, now what do you mean to accuse me of?"

"I accuse you of nothing but wasting precious time. I can have soldiers on his heels in five minutes, but..." he hesitated.

"But... It's always but," said the large woman.

141

"But, our son is a man who makes his own decisions."

"But I'm his mother and I have a say as I too am on the Mothertree Counsel."

"Yes, a position that was won on the bravery and strength of our son's accomplishments," his father went on.

Billy sat in awe at what he was seeing when a small bubble came from behind him and traveled in front of his face. He saw its insides glow and flow. A thought came into his mind. "It's time for you to go. This land is not to be yours just yet. See Mr. Caytoe. He will show you the way," the bubble said, bounced up and down in front of him and zipped off into the clear night.

Billy was startled and thought, "I want to go back to my body," and was transported there in a split second by an unseen force. He sat up. "They're alive!" he exhaled in a thunderous roar. Though he was excited, he forced himself to lie back down and close his eyes. A part of him wanted to go immediately back to his giant parents, but remembered the strange little bubble's words and slept lightly for the remainder of the night.

He heard his cousin Manny come quietly into the bedroom an hour later, but he kept his eyes closed. He didn't feel like sharing the experience with anyone just yet, if ever. He knew this wasn't something you revealed to just anyone and even though Manny was family, he was still a stranger to him. He couldn't trust anyone with something this extreme, especially something he didn't understand himself.

Seeing visions of his parents was one thing. People might be open to hearing that, especially if that person's parents recently passed, but how could he tell his aunt, cousin or anyone that he was able to go outside of his body and fly wherever he wanted?

Over the slowly moving minutes in the dark, Billy came to the conclusion that he would keep it a secret from his family, but would pay Mr. Caytoe a visit in the morning.

THIRTEEN

....

RU-ADO TRUSTS THE WATER

Ru-Ado walked away from the wounded human with a new respect towards their species, though he knew them to be horrible as well.

"Our life is in the hands of our choices," came a soft, but firm voice in his mind. His grandfather, the Sho-Han, always took the time to depart wisdom to Ru-Ado over the course of his seventeen winters, never knowing when the time would come for him to walk alone into the forest. The Sho-Han saw the potential in his oldest grandson.

Ru-Ado listened to the Sho-Han, but only to a certain degree. He had become only interested in his own thoughts and dreams of leading a new tribe of zuzuans, away from the rules of his ancestors.

His mind went back to the human and thought that he might try and climb out of the hole as soon as he could, but he never made a sound. He stayed where he was and Ru-Ado let him be.

He continued on throughout the day and the wound on his leg became worse and worse as the day progressed. By sundown Ru-Ado was reduced to feeling a dull, but sharp pain shoot up his leg and back every time he took a step. Flies were constantly present, no matter how often he tried to shoo them away, but he forced himself to forget about them. He knew that he must find water soon to clean the wound.

He saw a decline in his path and knew that there would be water in the small valley ahead. The moonlight replaced the sun by the time Ru-Ado found a river large enough for him to sit down and clean his wound thoroughly. He felt feverish and unclear. He sat his large body in the water and brought his hand down to the wound. As soon as his finger touched the skin he recoiled in pain.

He sat there for a long time and just let the water run over the gash in his leg until his skin had pruned, got up and walked carefully over to a cluster of ferns and lay down on them. His fever grew hotter and sweat poured out of his body. Ru-Ado had never been this ill and did not know what to do. "Sho-Han, please show me how to heal," he thought and he let out a weak howl.

A deeply graveled voice came from all around him. "RU-ADO... I can soothe your fear. I can heal your wounds. I too was of the Zuzuan Tribe, but was falsely confined. I need the strongest and most courageous warriors to help me escape this eternal prison. I will heal your wounds and you will serve all zuzuan by restoring our throne to power. This was our world once and it will be again if... you let me help you," the voice said and trailed off.

Ru-Ado mustered every ounce of strength he had, stood to his full thirteen-foot frame and extended his mighty arms high while roaring longer and louder than he ever had in his entire life.

"I am Ru-Ado and I fear no one. I will heal myself. Leave me now!" he roared again and charged forward into a large tree in front of him, knocking it down to the ground. He stood and looked all around him. "I can see my brothers. I can feel the hair on their bodies," he hallucinated.

Ru-Ado's strength had run out and his massive body fell to the ground unconscious, forcing his needed sleep. When he woke up in the morning he was very thirsty, but felt weaker than ever. He walked slowly on all fours back to the river and let himself fall in. The water immediately cooled his body and after a little while, some of the effects of the fever. When he had the strength, he sat up and looked around him for herbs on the riverbank.

The Sho-Han and his father, Ado-Han had shown him which plants were poisonous and others that could heal an injury, but he saw none that were familiar to him. It was not often he traveled this far away from the tribe's home hunting grounds and never alone. Crows landed on both sides of the riverbanks and surrounded Ru-Ado. He scowled at the birds and said, "I'm not dead yet! Go away!" scaring the birds off of the ground and onto near-by trees.

He grunted low "Not dead yet," and closed his eyes, feeling the energy of the water coarse through his body. He let the steady sound take his pain away. He repeated over and over. "Heal me... Heal me... Heal me," his low voice was drowned out by the sound of the water.

A surge of power went through him faster than the crack of a thunder-stick and his body took what it needed from the water. When the sun made its way past the roof of the trees above him, he got up much stronger than before and hungry once again.

While Ru-Ado had been meditating he heard large fish swimming with the current of the water. He had once been successful catching a large amount of blue-skinned fish by trapping them into a shallow bank, so that is what he did. Walking upright, but slow to conserve his energy, Ru-Ado walked to the tree he felled just a few hours ago and dragged it by its heavy base to create a false path for the fish to follow. Ru-Ado would simply have to wait for each small meal to come, but he would eat.

He walked a short distance from his spot at the river's bend and found what he was looking for, a group of tall, but young trees. He reached high on the thinnest of them and pulled back gently, as not to break it. Then pulled another over to the first, hooking the two together by large branches up top.

He repeated the process with three others, making the five bent trees look like a long, but uncovered tee-pee. Its purpose was to tell any other zuzuan in the area that this land had been claimed and all trespassers beware. Ru-Ado looked up with some pride at his work. He was feeling stronger and stronger by the minute and was grateful for some relief.

He walked back over to the river to see if his trap had worked and was happy to discover two large trout struggling to turn around in the shallow water against a strong current. Ru-Ado almost ran over to the fish with want and hunger, but controlled himself. He quickly caught one with his long fingers and put half of the fish in his mouth headfirst. He chewed with delight as he devoured the fresh meat. He ate the rest of the fish in one more large bite and chewed thoroughly. He saw the second fish trying to flee, but it was tired from swimming so long without a rest. Ru-Ado picked it up easily and ate it too.

Sated for the moment, but still very hungry Ru-Ado looked for a better place to sleep than on top of the large ferns. He wanted a place to provide some sort of cover. Even though he was an ominous fighter, he was wounded and didn't want to take any more chances.

It was his luck that he found exactly what he was looking for only a short distance away from the river. Halfway up a hill on the other side of the river. He found a cave that was big enough for three zuzuan warriors to sleep and was partially covered by fallen trees and vines that had grown over them.

Inside was a bed of moss thick enough to ease his injured body. He walked over to another fallen tree and placed it over the rest of his cave, leaving just enough room for him to come in and out of with ease. Ru-Ado did not plan on staying in this land very long, but made the best of it.

He walked back over to the fish trap and was once again pleased to find three more large trout scrambling in the shallows. He grunted with pleasure as he walked over to his next meal, but was stopped in his tracks by a noise that sounded like a fleet of locusts. Ru-Ado heard it getting closer and closer until he saw what it was.

Just over the treetops came a metal bird flying slowly over the branches. It sailed by without stopping and disappeared over another group of taller trees. Ru-Ado tried to follow it, but it moved too swiftly for him. Any other day he might even think of climbing these trees to knock it out of the air, but today he just allowed himself the curiosity.

He had seen these metal birds many times in winters past, but they never harmed him. He began to see them as just another rare creature in the forest. He never really gave them much thought until now and it was gone quickly.

It came back again, this time coming closer to him and held at a hover just above. Wind from the metal bird's belly shot into Ru-Ado's face, pushing at his thick white mane of hair.

He looked to the ground for a stone to throw at it, but when he finally stood back up with a boulder in hand, the metal bird was gone. He held onto the stone and brought it with him to the fish trap, placing it on the log. If it came back, he would be ready.

FOURTEEN

TAKESHI SAYS GOOD-BYE

Takeshi climbed the fallen tree with the skill and dexterity of a drunken monkey. Though his ankle and ribs felt much better than a few days ago, he was still very sore. The bark on the dying tree was slippery from the recent rain and made it difficult for him to maintain balance as he pulled from limb to limb.

Once at the top he stepped off of the tree and lowered himself onto wet leaves covering firm ground. He looked down at his former death trap, spit into the gash in the Earth and without saying a word, he instinctively began to limp back towards his father's home.

Flashes of his old life began to cross his vision; baseball training, morning noon and night for the rest of his life and a father who could not see past his own glory. Takeshi stopped in his tracks and looked to the ground. "I promised myself that I would go to Mt. Shasta to find my purpose. Why am I walking home?" he thought and in a second he knew the answer. "Because it's easy and I'm tired," he said aloud.

He closed his eyes and remembered Ishmael. "I will go to Mt. Shasta and see what the forest brings. I will miss Coach Mattingly and will always remember his words, but there will be others who need him more than me," he said with real meaning. He looked up the hill that would lead him back home and said, "Good-bye, Father. I'll see you in another life." He turned around and walked in the direction of Mt. Shasta.

Little did Takeshi know that as he began his trek to Mount Shasta, his father, Hiro, had just flown onto the landing strip behind his family estate.

Six men in San Francisco Giants wind jackets stood on the tarmac waiting for him. They watched the slender dark-skinned man walk toward them. His tight muscles showed through his blue button-down shirt and tailored silk pants.

The senior of the group approached Hiro first. He wore aviator sunglasses and a stern expression. "Mr. Nakano, I'm sorry, but we still haven't located your son. I think we might need to call in for additional help. I can have the local authorities over here in ten minutes, just give me the word," he said.

"Thank you, Mr. Woodcock, but I prefer to keep the matter private. I have more than enough resources available to me at the moment. It is only a matter of time until we find him. I have sent out several military-grade drones into our surrounding area, programmed to record everything they see. I have also ordered my entire staff of fifty men and women to scour the local woods."

"I'm sorry, Sir, I didn't mean to imply anything," said Mr. Woodcock. A bit of the severity drained from his face. He knew of Hiro Nakano's reputation as a no-nonsense man and did not want to give his boss the wrong impression.

Hiro saw the man's change in expression and made him feel better. "Thank you for all of your help, Mr. Woodcock. I truly appreciate it and know your intentions, but I'll take of the matter from here," he said.

"Yes, Sir, thank you, Sir." Mr. Woodcock said and walked back to his previous position, watching the man walk calmly back to his home. He leaned in to talk with another San Francisco Giant employee, "That man has ice running through his veins," he said low enough only for the man to hear. The smaller and more nervous employee just nodded his head up and down, not wanting to revel his inner thoughts to his senior.

"Ice in his veins," Woodcock repeated just to hear his own voice.

As soon as Hiro walked through the doors of his bedroom and into his personal shower he took a deep breath as the warm water from the shower head hit his face, he held it and released in one long exhale. "I will not show remorse for something that did not happen. I know my son will survive. I have absolute faith and will not give myself to worry," he said as he took another long breath and exhaled. He washed his body thoroughly and changed into a comfortable jumpsuit. He exited his bedroom door and was immediately greeted by an elderly Japanese man waiting outside.

"Ohio, Hiro-san," said Yoshi Yamaguchi, Hiro's oldest and most trusted employee. He held out a cup of tea for Hiro.

"Ohio, Yoshi-san. Domo," he said, took the cup from the older man and walked out of the house to the small security building on his estate. He opened the door and ten men stood to attention.

"Good morning gentlemen. Is there anything you can tell me about my son?" Hiro said and took a sip of his tea.

None of the men wanted to speak first, but the security Chief knew his place. "Mr. Nakano, Sir, We haven't seen hide nor hair of him. Yet," he quickly added, "but if he's out there, the drones are going to find him," he said, waiting nervously for his employer's response.

Another security guard stepped forward, finding the courage. He had wispy blond hair and thick glasses that covered a good portion of his face. "Sir, just to let you know that these drones have the ability to categorize everything they see and send that information back to us immediately. We have found six black bears, twenty-three deer and one hundred thirty-three squirrels."

Hiro looked at his junior employee with dislike. Even though the man gave him good information, he had stepped over his chain of command. In Hiro's eyes he had disrespected his senior. He ignored the man and turned back to the Chief.

The Chief coughed nervously, not knowing the reason for the tension, but carried on. "Sir, we did find

159

an anomaly that concerned us. It has nothing to do with Takeshi, but..." he hesitated.

Hiro's eyes opened wide. "Enough talk, show me now," he said with agitation. The Chief silently gestured for the blonde security guard to open the screen for viewing. He touched a file with his finger and a video showed a huge albino ape-like creature standing in the river. The creature saw the drone and was about to throw a boulder at the drone, but the video ended, leaving a still image of the beast in full view.

"We saw the potential for danger and got the drone out of there before he could throw that rock at it."

"What is it?" Hiro asked, trying to cover his amazement.

The Chief saw that the younger security guard was about to speak up again and interjected, "We think it might be a Sasquatch, Sir. You know, a Bigfoot?" he said and waited for the worst.

Hiro wanted to call foul, but was staring right at the creature. It lived right on his property. "Call all Nakano staff back to the guardhouse immediately, we cannot put any more lives in danger. That animal will kill a man without trying."

The Chief was surprised and spoke out of line. "What about Takeshi, Sir?" he said with passion.

Hiro sighed, "Takeshi will survive," he said, looking at the screen once more for a long time before walking out of the guard shack and back to his home without saying another word.

Takeshi sat on the edge of a log and took off his sneakers very carefully. They were pressing so tightly that it felt like his feet were about to burst from the fabric. Once free, the pain in his feet and toes diminished almost completely except for the constant low-grade pain in his right ankle. He let the sneakers drop to the ground and wiggled his toes gratefully. When he took his socks off of his feet he knew something was wrong. His once bronze skin was undeniably blue. "Was it the water from the cave?" he said and took off all of his clothes to inspect his entire body. It was undeniable. His skin had indeed changed to a light blue color. He looked at the muscles on his body and saw definition and mass like never before. Though he had always been in great shape since he was allowed to begin his training at five years old, but the changes he had gone through in the last four days had outmatched his last ten years.

There was no real way of him telling, but he thought he had grown no less than six inches. Everything about him seemed bigger and blue. "Have you done this to me, Ishmael? Is this who I really am?" he said aloud.

From the distance a great bellow blasted through the air. Takeshi turned to it and froze. It was the same roar that screamed down on him the day before. Takeshi put his wet jump suit on as quickly as he could, but knew that the monster was not yelling at him. He found a sharp stone on the ground and cut holes in the front his sneakers and put them back on his feet. They wore like opened-toed sandals and he was glad that the incoming weather from the ocean had been warmer than the previous days. He wiggled his big blue toes and had to laugh at himself.

The beast roared again and wiped the smile from his face. He hid behind a large rock sticking out of the ground and waited to hear it again before moving from behind the boulder. After ten minutes in a crouched position his muscles ached from inaction. He stood carefully as he walked from his hidden position to look for water and shelter. He was upwind from the Sasquatch and knew he would be able to camp for the night in relative safety.

162

He breathed deeply and sme led water coming from the bottom of a narrow valley, in the same direction as the Sasquatch. "If I walk parallel to the river for a half mile, I'll be able to camp near water and away from that Bigfoot," he said to himself. He walked for another thirty minutes through the densely packed forest until he found a perfect spot next to the water.

A large elm tree hung a huge branch over the river bank just high enough for Takeshi to line it with long sticks and then as much reed grass as he could build upon it. He eased himself on the makeshift bed and felt comfort like never before. The branch held him as securely as a mother to infant child.

Happy with his sleeping arrangements, Takeshi fought his tiredness and lowered himself from the tree hammock and began to look for food on the ground. Upon inspection of his immediate area he was quickly rewarded by finding another type of mushroom his father had called "chicken of the woods". Like the Oyster mushrooms, they grew in abundance on dying trees. He bit into it expecting one flavor, but was instantly disappointed. "Not bad, but that's no chicken," he said and grimaced as he ate the remainder of the large orange crescent shaped mushroom.

He walked to the edge of the river and drank until his belly was full. He climbed back into the protection of his tree and swayed up and down with the wind, wondering about the Sasquatch.

"I'm going to try and talk to it," he thought. He knew it was a crazy idea, but he somehow also knew that the giant could be an ally, rather than an enemy. "He didn't try to kill me," he reasoned with himself, "and he turned his head when I spoke to him in Japanese. What if?" he said out loud, but the steady rushing of the river below carried off the words.

FIFTEEN

....

BILLY GETS A SURPRISE

Billy remembered the way back to Manny's secret place and easily re-traced their steps from a day before. Billy walked much slower this time, wanting to absorb the scenery in a pace he enjoyed. He spread his arms out wide and ran his fingers through the tall grass and wild flowers, their smell overwhelming his senses once again. He picked a small pink flower and smelled its sweetness.

As he walked past the field and through the thicket of trees he saw nature as he always dreamed it would be; perfectly imperfect and absolutely beautiful. He loved the different birds chirping to their friends. Their whole existence was a mystery to him. "There's so much I don't know," he said out loud, listening to the truth in his words and stayed in thought for the rest of the walk to Mr. Caytoe's property.

He found the grapevine maze and walked it without any problems. He looked closer at how the vines grew and couldn't imagine how long it would take someone to weave these branches as precisely as they were.

He walked into the mysterious man's backyard and took in the beauty of the rest of his garden, every plant and color blending in with the next. Each a work of art within themselves, but collectively they made a masterpiece. Billy admired his way of life and loved the simplicity. "He doesn't need anyone or anything. He has it all right here," he said out loud and was immediately surprised.

"Not quite yet, but yes, I'm getting there," came a baritone voice from behind him.

Billy turned around to see Mr. Caytoe. "Uh, hello. My name is Billy and I live..." he said, but was cut-off.

"At the orchard down the road. My feline security system told me about your little visit yesterday," he said and smiled easily, amused by the boy. "My name is Caytoe," he winked and smiled. "Just don't call me mister," he said and laughed at his inside joke. He was impressed at how the boy held himself. There was no lie about him. He was unsure, but still sure. Caytoe knew he was going to like him.

Billy found the courage to speak up. "You can talk to cats?" he asked, wide-eyed.

"Yes," he said with a smile, "cats, dogs, birds and plants." He looked up and thought, "I can't quite understand humans." He laughed at himself and Billy joined in.

"How did you learn to speak with them?" Billy asked.

"Years and years of watching and listening. If you know how something lives without your getting involved, then communication becomes pretty easy," he said.

"Years?" Billy asked.

"Sometimes no, but mostly yes."

"Could you show me, Caytoe?"

"Hmm..." Caytoe thought, but Billy interjected before he could finish.

"I had a crazy sort of dream last night and at the end of it a voice told me to come see you. I know that sounds weird, but..." he trailed-off.

"Weird?" Caytoe laughed. "That's the best reference you could give me. Follow me, I'll show you right now," Caytoe said walking ahead of the boy without waiting for his response. Billy followed Caytoe over to the far end of his garden where a circle of citrus trees was grouped together in huddle.

At the far edge of the circle there was a tangerine tree with new growth sticking out from the rest of the intertwined branches. Caytoe walked up to the stray twigs. "Excuse me my friend, but I've noticed that your new shoots are running far away from your circle. Would you mind tucking your branches in with the others?" he asked loud enough for Billy to hear. In front of their eyes, the branches wiggled and turned into the rest of the tree growth as if it always belonged.

"That's incredible," Billy said while trying to contain his excitement in front of his new teacher.

"It's really just a partnership with the Universe," Caytoe said with a chuckle.

The boy was perplexed. "What do you mean?" he questioned.

"I mean that I can see and understand the bigger picture in all things. The Universe can only give you what you have the ability to see and feel. I saw an image in my mind of the tree in a perfect circle and expressed to the tree in my words and feelings that it would be to their benefit to create that vision of perfection for me," he said.

"Is it that simple?" Billy asked.

"Sometimes. Sometimes it takes a lot more effort, but only in creating that perfect picture. The Universe only knows how to respond to our vision," Caytoe said. He looked at the boy again for a long time, studying his face and body.
"You look very much like your parents, do you know that?" he said and smiled.

Billy's look changed from wonder to confusion. "How do you know my parents?" he questioned.

"We were childhood friends," said Caytoe.

"You were?"

"Yes, my parents used to own this property before me," Caytoe said, looking around his land.

"They died?" Billy asked.

"A long time ago," said Caytoe.

"Mine died a couple of days ago," Billy said and turned his head to the ground.

"I know, I was sorry to hear it," he said, pausing a long time, keeping his stare just over Billy's head.

Billy raised his head and broke the silence. "I saw them last night in my dream too," he said, a bit brighter.

Caytoe's eyes opened wide and gazed intensely at the boy. "Really? How *big*... was the experience for you?" he said and smiled brightly.

"They were giants! *You* saw them too?" Billy asked, stunned.

"No, I didn't see them, but I know they exist. I saw their son, Tem and his grandfather in the forest," he said.

"Tem! That's his name, I heard them talking about him," Billy said and added, "What forest? This one?" Billy pointed to the woods just beyond Caytoe's property.

"No... it's a bit more difficult than that," Caytoe chuckled.

"How?" asked Billy, disheartened.

"That particular forest is not on the Earth. It's hundreds of miles under it."

"They live inside the Earth?" Billy eyes opened wide.

"Yes," Caytoe said as a matter of fact.

"But there was a moon in the sky just like ours and stars in the sky."

"Yes, but what does that mean?" asked Caytoe.

"I don't know. It just seemed wrong somehow."

172

"What is right? What is wrong?"

"I uh, don't know."

"Exactly. Ultimately, we decide what is right or wrong for us," Caytoe said, getting excited about the conversation.

"We do?"

"Yes, we do. We are the captain of our own ships navigating this thing we call life based on a series of yes's or no's that we agree to believe in."

"Wow! You're a really smart man."

"No, I just choose to *believe* I'm smart." Caytoe smiled brightly and they both laughed a long time.

"Why did you go the forest to see Tem and uh, his grandfather?" Billy asked after the laughter died down.

"Because of you," Caytoe said.

"Me?"

"You're not the only one who has *weird* dreams, kiddo." He emphasized the word *weird* and winked at Billy.

"You do too?"

"Of course, but they are not what you think of as dreams," Caytoe said. His face changed again and looked serious.

"Then what are they?" Billy asked.

173

"The experience is called going out of your body."

"That's what I saw!" Billy said, now excited. "I saw myself floating out of my body."

"But you were still there, right?" Caytoe questioned.

"Yes, but I could see through my skin," Billy added.

"Of course," said Caytoe.

"Why did you go to see... the other me?" Billy asked.

"Very good, Billy, you learn quickly. I didn't ask to see him," Caytoe said.

His big white cat, Hathor, strolled over to them to say hello by rubbing against the back of Caytoe's legs. Caytoe kneeled down and silently rubbed his friend's coat of thick fur. He looked back up to Billy. "I knew your parents died because I felt it inside of me. They were the only friends I knew for a long time and they were a big part of my life." He let a tear fall and wiped it away. "In the same way that I knew your parents were gone from this place, I also knew that you would be coming to Tangerine Park. All I did was ask the Universe to show me how I would be able to help you," he said.

Billy didn't know what to say, but still managed, "Thank you, but you still didn't tell me what you saw," he asked, keeping Caytoe on task.

"It appears that you need to make a very important choice."

"About what?"

"About staying here." He pointed around him. "Or going... there," he said.

SIXTEEN

TEM LEARNS THE HARD WAY

Tem moved quickly down the wide city streets. Hovering globes of light illuminated his path off of the pyramid and into the darkened jungle.

Chica flew behind him every step of the way, making sure not to lose his friend. So much ran through his little mind that he couldn't tell his friend. They were comrades in life and were dedicated to each other. If Tem needed him not to question his actions he would do just that; he was bound by the closeness of their friendship.

Chica was a nervous bird to begin with, but having to help manage such an adventurous friend was taking its toll on him. He was startled easily when a howl came from the east. It was the call of the

177

zuzuan and every citizen in Bubble Valley knew it well. Another call came from the south.

"Tem, did you hear that?" peeped Chica, now on Tem's shoulder.

"Don't bother me with this now, Chica, zuzuans do not frighten me, remember?" Tem said with courage.

"But they frighten *me...*" squeaked Chica.

"Everything frightens you!" Tem laughed loud, not caring who heard.

"At least you could lower your voice a little," Chica said as he looked around in the darkness.

"OK, just leave me alone. Promise?" Tem said laughing at his friend, but Chica didn't respond. "Promise?" Tem said, a little louder.

"OK, I promise, I promise. Just shut your big mouth," Chica said in a low, sing-song voice. Tem chuckled again and continued to run through the thicket of trees, blind without light.

Chica saw a large branch jutting down from above that looked to be lined up with Tem's head. He thought of chirping loudly to help his friend, but hesitated for a second, remembering his threat. He was about to warn him but was too late. His beak was stuck open wide as Tem ran directly into the branch, knocking him out cold.

"Tem!" Chica squawked. He flew quickly to his lifeless body and hovered above him. "Oh, you big idiot! I told you to be careful. I really don't know what to think about being your adviser any longer. Why bother? You never listen anyway," he said as he zoomed around his body to see if he was bleeding. "At least you're not too badly hurt, but what am I going to tell your parents?" he said remembering. "Your parents! They're going to pluck my feathers out and eat me for breakfast for not protecting you. Oh my, Mothertree, what should I do?" he worried.

Another howl thundered around them, then another immediately after. Chica knew they were closing in and there was nothing he could do about it besides watch the most horrendous site imaginable.

Chica saw two monstrously ravenous zuzuans step out of the woods and into the clearing of the well-worn path. He couldn't make out their color, but was frozen with fear by staring at their red glowing eyes.

They walked forward quickly toward the unconscious Tem, for them an easy meal, but a series of loud crashes through brush revealed several of Tem's personal guards. They ran in front of their leader to protect his body from the zuzuans and held long golden axes high, ready for battle.

The zuzuans were not afraid of the men, but knew when they were outmatched. They turned quickly and ran back into the forest.

Chica became brave as soon as they were out of sight, turning to the men in the group. "You are lucky you got here when you did, our Tem was almost eaten. How did you know to find us here?" he asked.

A young warrior, eleven feet tall with stark white hair and dark brown skin stepped forward. He was Tem's second in command. "We were informed by a stray first soul. The creature was freighted after the Earth-shake and sought refuge under Tem's bed. He overheard your conversation. That first soul saved your lives," he said, annoyed by the boisterous bird.

Befuddled by his reminder of humility, Chica turned his head quickly, sending his massive red plume of hair in a bobbing swirl. He corrected his temperament fast and told the warrior with dignity, "I am grateful for our lives. Thank you. I will certainly send word to the High Counsel of the Mothertree to honor your courage and bravery."

The warrior was happy with Chica's response and looked at his fallen leader. "What happened to him?" he asked.

"He ran into... this." He flew up above the warrior's head and pointed out the branch that knocked Tem out.

"Ah, is he OK?" the warrior asked.

"It seems, he's breathing," said Chica.

"Good! We're going to need him soon. Without him we'll certainly lose the Bubble Valley games to another tribe," said another warrior.

"Don't say that! You'll curse us," Chica spat in his direction.

"I'm sorry," was all that came out before Tem stirred beneath Chica.

"Oh..." he moaned. "My head." He brought his hand to his head to feel for blood and saw none.

"It serves you right for not listening to your trusted and most loyal adviser. I nearly gave my life to protect your sorry bottom. You were nearly eaten by zuzuan, you big oaf," Chica chastised.

"Eaten? Are you kidding?" Tem said, still groggy.

"No, if it weren't for your warriors here, you would have become a meal," Chica said. The white-haired warrior bent down to give Tem his hand. Tem grabbed it and pulled himself up.

"Thank you, brother. I owe you a life," he said with significance.

"Nonsense, brother. We have a duty to one another," said the warrior.

Tem's strength was growing by the second. "Yes, we do and I am grateful, but I am going to ask you another favor," said Tem.

"Anything," responded the warrior.

"Excellent. Have the men follow me to Tipereth. My grandfather might be in danger and we could use all the help we can get."

The warrior looked to him and then looked back at the others in the darkness. "We're in," he said loud enough for the men to hear.

"Good, now follow me," Tem said as a marching order. His men lined in single file behind him, walking at his pace. They were happy to be doing what they were trained and scoured the woods around them as they walked through the night.

By daybreak, Tem and his men had crossed into Tipereth, some of them for the first time and were a little nervous of the unknown lands. Tem saw the look on some of their faces and knew what they were thinking. "No worries, men, Tipereth is ancient and forbidding, but there is no need for fear. There is no fighting allowed in Tipereth. It is a pact as old as time between the tribes and the Mothertree," he said continuing on into the forest, feeling confident and alive.

By mid-afternoon Tem saw what he'd hoped he would never have to, his grandfather, Ishmael, dead on the ground in front of a beautiful pinecone statue.

He called out, "Grandfather!" as he threw himself to the ground and on top of Ismael; tearing the vines from his old body. Before Chica or any of the warriors could say a word, the mighty Tem had fallen. His body lay slumped against Ishmael's, still holding the vines in his grasp.

The white-haired warrior who was just a few steps away held up his hands up and hollered, "Stop! Don't touch them!" The men behind him halted in their tracks and stared in amazement at their fallen leader.

Chica chirped loudly, "Tem! Master Ishmael!" He flew over their lifeless bodies. "Oh dear Mothertree, what a horror!" he said as tears ran down his feathery face.

The white-haired warrior bent over Tem and looked at his hands, then over to Ishmael. "The vines

183

are poisonous." He scanned the area, "Someone get me a long sturdy stick," he called out.

The most junior of his men broke from the pack and Chica flew ahead of him. "Over here, there's a branch over here," called Chica.

The warrior ran over and picked up a twenty-foot branch, holding it by the broken end and then back to Tem. He carefully removed the vines from Tem's fingers and with his other hand reached over his shoulder to a holstered long sword and cut the vine over Ishmael's head. He then used the branch to remove the remaining vines and flowers from their bodies. "Help me drag them away from this cursed statue," he barked, but the men were not as forthcoming this time. They all remained silent and unmoving. "Is there not one of you who will help our brother? He may still be alive," he hollered in anger. Chica flew to Tem and took his little finger into his miniature talons, hoisted himself up with great effort and flapped his wings feverishly. A swarthy youth of seventy-five, with bright orange hair stepped forward in consent.

"Thank you, Allister, I knew I could count on you," said the white-haired warrior, proud of his friend's courage. Shamed, the other soldiers quickly followed him to the fallen men.

"Grab his left leg. I'll take the right," the second in command said. Allister nodded. His eyes looked nervous, but he did as he was told.

"Carry the old man out of here behind us and be careful of the vines," the warrior said to his remaining men.

"Feel for their pulse," Chica ordered.

The second in command looked at the bird like he wanted to squish him in his big hands. Chica squawked loudly at the man's expression and flew high above him in fear of attack. The warrior talked under his breath and gently placed Tem's leg on the ground. "Put him down here," he said to Allister, brought his knee to the ground and put his fingers on Tem's jugular vein. "He's alive, but barely," he said with glee.

Everyone's eyes brightened. "Hooray!" came a chorus from the men.

"Be quiet you fools! Do you not remember the zuzuans from last night?" reprimanded the second in command.

The men remembered themselves and looked sheepish, but said nothing. The white-haired warrior

185

then put his finger to the neck of the old man and hung his head low, shaking it from side to side. They all were stunned into silence. He raised his head and spotted Chica. "You, bird, come here," he ordered.

Chica hesitated, "You won't hurt me?" he said, unsure.

"I won't hurt you. I'm going to put you to work," he said and smiled with tight lips. Chica flew down to the man slowly.

"I want you to fly back to the city and inform Tem's parents what has happened. Tell them I will have a medicine man ready for us."

Chica perked up. "You can count on me," he said as he flew over Tem's face. "It's going to be alright, my friend," and zipped off in-between the trees and into the open air. The men circled Tem and picked him up over their heads and rested his body on their broad shoulders.

"Alright men, everyone ready?" said the second in command and the men grumbled in response. "Off with your left and...march," he ordered. The warriors carried off Tem and Ishmael without another word. The magnitude of what had happened finally sinking in.

SEVENTEEN

....

TAKESHI IS SPOTTED

Over the course of the next two days Takeshi learned a lot more about what it was going to take for him to successfully live in the forest without the need of anyone else.

On the first morning near his convenient little hammock on the river's nook, Takeshi spent it looking for food besides mushrooms. He knew it didn't make any sense, but he thought he might be experiencing these body changes simply because of the food he was choosing to eat.

Of course he'd eaten all sorts of varieties of mushrooms in his life, including Oyster mushrooms and hadn't ever had an allergic reaction before. He bent down to roll over a log to look for grubs and readied himself to push very hard, but as soon as he gave his most minor of efforts the log rolled over easily.

"Whoa!" he said and pulled back the sleeves of his jump suit to look at his arms. "That's incredible," he said, stunned at the rippling blue-skinned muscles. He flexed and watched his arm muscles expand and contract as he moved them up and down. They looked like small, blue mountains. He pulled his sleeves back down and realized that they only extended to the middle of his forearms.

Takeshi suddenly had a burning desire to see his face, something he had been trying to avoid since he'd seen his skin turning color. He jogged over to the riverbank and noticed that he did not feel any pain from his previous wounds.

He stopped and slowly rotated his ankle three hundred and sixty degrees and felt no pain. He pressed his ribs gently with his fingers, then with a little more pressure. There was no pain.

"I'm completely healed," he said and wore a huge smile as he walked the remaining distance to the river. He decided to take off his clothes so he could go in the water to wash as well as use the water's reflective surface as a mirror. He walked in carefully and felt the coolness on his skin immediately. A ripple of energy rose up his back as he looked down into the water and saw a blue giant staring back at him. His mouth opened in awe at the sight of his new body.

Though his face was quite blue it remained unchanged, but his once jet black hair had turned completely silver, as brilliant and shining as any hair color he had yet to see. His father's son was still within the hulk of a man he saw in front of him, but he was fading fast.

He realized that he couldn't go back to his old life, even if he wanted to. The only world he had ever known would see him as a freak and something other than a man. His want to find what awaited him at Mount Shasta grew within him even more as his old life and looks melted away, but something held him to this place and somehow knew that the albino Sasquatch was important to him.

He scooped water into his hand and washed his body as best he could, when a whirring sound came over the tree line. It only took Takeshi a second to know what that sound was. Having been a remote control plane and helicopter enthusiast, he knew the sounds of even the most sophisticated equipment.

Takeshi did not want to wait for the drone to spot him first so he walked as fast as he could over

191

the slippery river rocks towards the safety of the tree line, but he wasn't fast enough. The drone spotted him and hovered above.

Back at Takeshi's home, Hiro began to show an uncharacteristically short temper. Though he was known for his quick emotionless orders, he rarely was impatient with those who worked for him. He was a strict, but a good boss to work for every day before this one. It had been fifty-two hours since he'd arrived home from his global tour promoting the San Francisco Giants' World Series victory. He'd left at a moment's notice once he'd gotten the word from Coach Mattingly, who was scheduled to oversee Takeshi's batting practice the Monday morning after the holidays. Today, Hiro had become furious with the now five drones recording every inch of his property.

"Sir! Maybe he hasn't gone where you think he has. Is it possible that he just has some girlfriend close by?" said a sleepy guard who had been up for nearly forty-eight hours straight.

Hiro fired him on the spot, for no more reason than the man's insolence to think that his son would disrespect his family and the effort that was put into his life.

"Takeshi is back there, I know it in my heart. I'm done relying on machines to do the work of a man. I'm going after my son, beast or no beast," he finally said to himself, alone in his bedroom. His shame was great and he knew it.

"Boom, boom, boom," came from his large wooden door.

Though briefly startled he sat up in bed, "Come!" he said loud enough for anyone to hear. His doors opened to reveal the Chief of the security guards.

"Mr. Nakano, we've found something. It looks like Takeshi," his eyes bright, but worried.

"Takeshi?" Hiro said and snapped out of bed in one leap, following the Chief back to the security shed. On the large monitor in the middle of the workroom was a still image of what seemed to be his son, but much larger in size and bulk. His skin was dark blue and his hair was bright silver. Hiro looked at the screen in disbelief. "This is not my son! Is this some kind of sick joke?" he snapped at the Chief.

Taken aback, the Chief didn't know how to respond to the grief stricken father. "Sir, would you like to see the video? I can assure you that it is no trick. This is the raw image video that came back from one of our drones just a few hours ago. We've spent these last hours scrutinizing every aspect of this video before we thought to even bother you with it," he finished.

Hiro nodded at the man's words and understood his commitment to him. "Thank you for your deep consideration Chief, please let me see the video," he said more somber. The Chief motioned to his new employee at the video console, who pressed the play button. Hiro watched the drone flying over a group of trees and then an open river. In the middle of the river was a humanoid that looked like Takeshi.

The Chief spoke up just as the video stopped. "Sir, we also have a few more video clips of the albino Sasquatch in the river. It seems there are a lot of strange looking creatures out there," he said, hoping his boss would not lose his temper on him again, but Hiro said calmly, "Chief, I am going to find my son. I will not be relying on drones any longer to do my job. Keep one of them in the air until I get back, but that's it," he said with finality.

"But, Sir!" the Chief started, but Hiro wouldn't hear anyone's words. He returned to his room and dressed for a scouting mission. Hiro had spent his entire childhood in the woods camping with his father, who was a Japanese military officer. Hiro armed himself with several large caliber handguns and walked into the woods alone.

Takeshi knew the drones were his father's and in a small way disliked him a little less for at least making some effort to find him. Nonetheless, he walked back to his hidden hammock and stayed there until nightfall. He knew the drones would be fitted with infrared cameras, but it just made him feel a little safer in the darkness. This was one of the many new things in his life that he was happy for. Darkness brought anonymity and right now he wanted as much of it as he could get.

Just before the sun went down Takeshi heard the Bigfoot chanting gruff words into the air and wondered what he was up to. He listened closely as the last of the light left the day. Tonight he would need to be brave and he knew it.

As soon as the sun went over the treetops, the forest became a private haven once again. He walked parallel to the river towards the sounds of chanting for a half of a mile and saw the Bigfoot sitting in the water with his eyes closed and singing words to a god unseen.

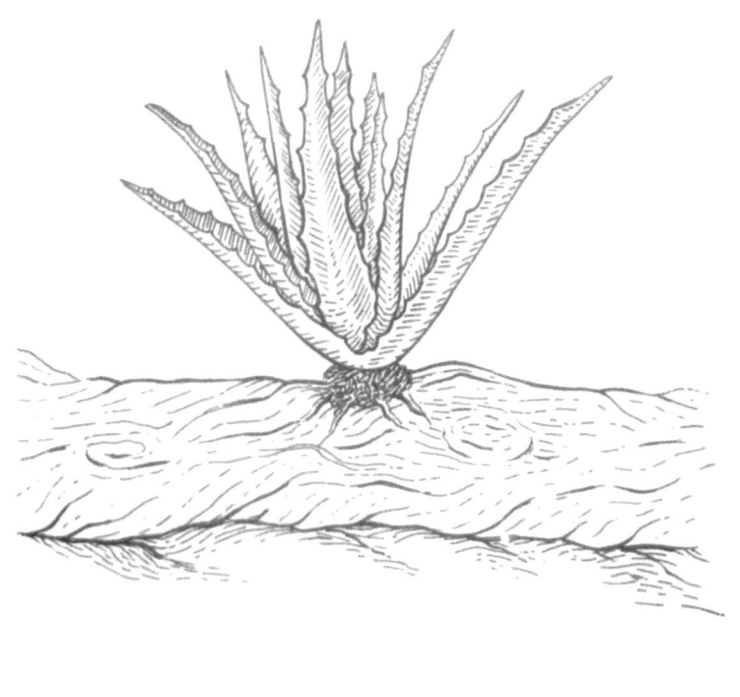

....

EIGHTEEN

RU-ADO MAKES A FRIEND

Ru-Ado sat in his cave behind the fallen tree and slowly ate the four large river fish he brought into his little temporary home. He was glad to have his privacy after having seen the metal bird. Something about it made him feel uneasy.

From deeper within the recesses of the cave came, "Ru-Ado... Ru-Ado..." called the familiar voice.

Ru-Ado turned around and felt violated by the intrusion. "Be gone spirit, I will not talk to you," he roared into the void.

"But, Ru-Ado... You haven't heard my offer. I see you have learned to heal your own wounds, but I have something much more enticing for you to ponder."

"I said be gone!" he roared even louder.

"I will do as you wish, Ru-Ado, but before I go I will tell you this," his demonic voice echoing off of the cave walls. "I offer you, Ru-Ado, total rule over all. You are to be the Zo-Han," the last of his words drifting back into the darkness.

Ru-Ado stared into the space from where the voice came for a long time, angry at the spirit's persistence, but even more because it knew his fondest wishes.

To be Zo-Han meant that he would have total rule over all zuzuan tribes and all of their leaders, including his father, Ado-Han, who would have to answer to *him*. To many other zuzuan warriors, this would be enticement enough to do whatever bidding was asked of them, but for Ru-Ado it was without honor. He would earn the rank without the help of anyone.

Ru-Ado stood up and walked to his makeshift doorway, sniffed outside the cave and smelled the human not too far away. He was curious, but not enough to waste his needed energy. He knew the human was no danger to him and walked back to the river slowly and listened to the morning speak.

He stepped into the river and sat down with a great splash. For a brief moment the water around him nearly vanished in a small tidal wave, but was quickly refilled. The tops of his thighs were just under the water, making it easy for him to see the gash created by the long since eaten boar. The cut was clean and it no longer oozed yellow. Ru-Ado lay his hand on top of the healing gash and felt much less pain than before, but it was still there.

He closed his eyes and repeated, "I am Ru-Ado, the greatest warrior of them all; I heal at my own demand." He had not heard these words before, but felt the power of them as the water rushed over his body.

After a while he felt something watching him and opened his eyes. It was the human staring at him from in-between the bushes lined at the river's bank. The sight of the human confused him because it had grown considerably. His entire body had turned blue and his hair was shining like the metal bird.

His eyes met Takeshi's. "Leave me alone," he grunted softly and closed his eyes again. He hoped that he wouldn't have to kill the human, especially since he had shown it mercy once before. After a few minutes he opened his eyes again and saw that the blue figure wasn't there any longer.

He thought, "I wonder if this human is one of the people who live under the mountain?" He knew that they had once been allies with the Zuzuan and thought that this human could be one of them. "Soon I will be strong enough to travel and I will see what he does. I will visit him tonight to see what he is made of. If he dies by my hand, he is not one of them. If he lives, I will let him travel with me to the Sacred Grounds."

Ru-Ado stayed in the water much longer than he had done over his previous visits to the river for want to complete his recovery. Though he enjoyed the constant supply of fresh fish, he wanted badly the taste of fresh elk or deer.

Ru-Ado got out of the river and walked to his fish trap to see if any more had been trapped while he was in the water and discovered only one fish, but saw something that was out of place on the fallen tree that created the fish trap. It was the long pointed plant that the Sho-Han had used to heal wounds for his tribe. It had been pulled from the ground and placed on the tree. Ru-Ado sent a low call of thanks into the air. He knew with the use of this plant on his cut, he would be ready to restart his trek to the Sacred Grounds and hopefully meet up with his father.

Though he felt less guilty, he still needed to leave his father with good intentions for the future. He picked up the fish and spiny plant by the roots and walked back to his cave to eat and rub the insides of the plant's thick leaves on his wound.

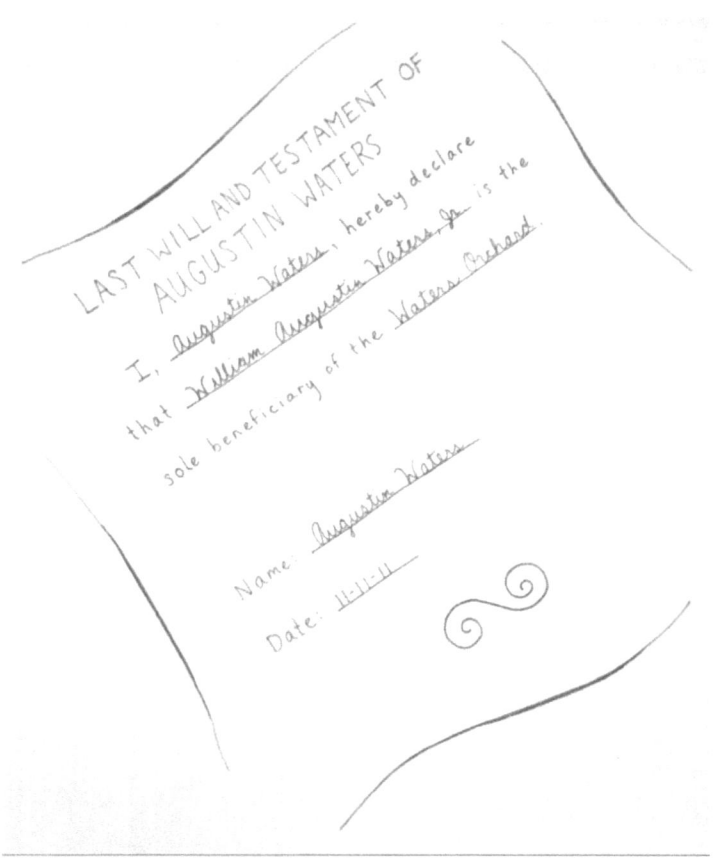

LAST WILL AND TESTAMENT OF
AUGUSTIN WATERS

I, Augustin Waters, hereby declare
that William Augustin Waters, Jr. is the
sole beneficiary of the Waters Orchard.

Name: Augustin Waters

Date: 11-11-11

202

NINETEEN

....

BILLY MEETS DON EDUARDO

Billy walked home from Caytoe's with a lot on his mind.

"I will do whatever it takes in this universe or any other to hold my parents again,' he said looking at another person's version of paradise. A young squirrel darted in front of him and onto a near-by tree. It shot straight up the large oak and into his nest.

"There's nothing for me here without them," he said and walked out of the woods and into the field of wild flowers separating the two properties.

From a crouch, Manny sprung up in front of him, hidden beneath the pungent plants. "So, you broke our code of trust already?" he said in a huff.

"WA...!" Billy screamed as he was shot out of his daydream. "Darn it, Manny! You nearly scared me to death. What are you spying on me?" he asked.

203

"How could I be spying on you? It's *my* hide-out," he said, clearly aggravated.

Billy shot back, "It's not yours, Manny," stunned by his own spark of anger. Manny looked at his cousin and realized the truth. He had to see it for what it was. "It's Mr. Caytoe's," Billy said, much softer.

"Yeah... I know, but, you know..." he said and turned his head to the ground. Tears fell down his face. "It's all I got," he said in a near whisper.

Billy looked at his cousin and was immediately sorry for snapping at him. "I'm sorry, Manny. I didn't mean it like that," he apologized.

"It's OK, Billy, you're only telling the truth. I know it's his. I just like to pretend, you know?" he paused, "that I have a place of my own where I can grow my own trees and not worry if Don Eduardo is always threatening to kick us out." His voice was monotone and emotionless.

Billy suddenly had a thought about his conversation with Aunt Maria, just before leaving for Caytoe's home and knew what to do. Aunt Maria had handed him an open yellow envelope that held the contents of his grandfather Augustin's will and found out that he was the new owner of the orchard directly adjacent to Don Eduardo's property. Though Aunt

204

Maria was excited for him, she didn't know what had happened to him just a few hours earlier. He told Maria that he would think about what he wanted to do with it and would let her know later. She was a little perplexed, but let it go as she knew this was a tough time for Billy.

Billy smiled at his cousin and told him what happened that morning and said, "I'm giving my grandfather Augustin's orchard to your mom and dad," and smiled bright.

"You're what?" Manny asked. shocked by Billy's statement.

"I'm giving your parents my house and orchard to run. I don't know what to do with it. I just want to have a home," he said, very sincere.

They walked past Don Eduardo's house and saw him staring at them through the screen door on his front porch. Manny looked at the screen and back to Billy. "Oh my God, Billy! Mom and dad are going to be so happy," he said low enough for just Billy's ears.

Billy looked at Don Eduardo's home with different eyes. He stared defiantly toward Don Eduardo and said, "Let's go tell them now. We can start moving tomorrow!" He ran ahead of Manny, truly happy for the first time in a very long time. Manny followed almost skipping as he ran. They arrived at Manny's house and opened the screen door to the kitchen, but were met at the door by Aunt Maria.

"Dios mio! Where have you boys been? I've been worried. Lunch has been ready for thirty minutes already," she said with motherly worry.

"I'm sorry, mom," said Manny with his head down.

"I'm sorry, Aunt Maria. It was my fault. Don't blame Manny. I went to his secret place without him and he went looking for me."

She changed her worry to concern. "Is everything all right?" she scanned their bodies for injury. "Are any of you hurt?" she asked.

"No, mom, we're great. Don't worry," Manny said as he remembered Billy's news. "Billy's got something to tell you." His face shone from excitement.

Maria stared at Billy curiously. "What is it sweet heart?" she asked.

Billy told Maria and something unexpected happened. She passed out on the floor.

Manny saw his mother drop and screamed, "Mom!" loud enough for his barely sober father to overhear, but ran to the porch to see what happened.

Uncle Carlos saw his wife out cold on the floor and ran over to her. "Maria!" he said, sobering up in a hurry, showing uncharacteristic love. "Maria, my love! Don't die on me. I couldn't live without you," he said as tears began to roll down his cheeks. One fell to his wife's face and on her chin.

Maria picked up her hand and wiped her chin free. "I'm glad to see that you still love me. I was beginning to wonder," she said, smiled and told her husband what Billy had just told her. He nearly fainted on top of his wife, but recovered just in time and straightened himself out.

He walked over to Billy and looked at him in the eyes for the first time since they met. "Thank you, mi hijo!" and hugged him like a son.

Billy let his uncle hug him, but pulled away quickly, feeling suddenly uncomfortable with all of the praise. "You're welcome, Uncle Carlos," he said and smiled uneasily.

"Knock, knock, Knock!" came at the screen door just as they all sat down to lunch. Aunt Maria cursed under her breath as she walked to the door and stood there in mild shock. "Father," she said with hesitation. "How can I help you?" she turned back to her family and said, "We just sat down to lunch and it's getting cold."

Don Eduardo blew out a great cloud of smoke from his cigar into the home through the screen. "I want to see my grandson and welcome him to my home," he said, waving his arms around in a grand gesture.

Maria looked at her father seriously and wondered what he was really up to. "He's eating lunch. I'll bring him to your house later," she said. She was about to close the door on him, but he screamed at the top of his lungs in a great fit of anger.

"How dare you close the door on me to my own home. You're lucky I let you live here," he said and pushed the door open, walking directly into the kitchen.

Billy stood up and saw the bully his mother had always told him about and was saddened by this first experience. "I'm sorry, Don Eduardo, but I really don't want to speak to you," he said as a matter of fact.

"What? How dare you talk to your grandfather like that?" he stuttered furiously.

"You're not my grandfather. You're my mother's father. My grandfather died and left me his orchard," he said and looked hard at the old man.

Don Eduardo straightened up and changed on the spot. "Listen, my little one. I know you're angry with me and I understand. I'm a complicated man. I get a little..." he pulled at his button down shirt collar "...hot under the collar sometimes. You've got to forgive an old man for bad habits," he said with no real meaning.

"There's nothing for us to talk about," Billy said confidently and sat back down to eat. He took a bite of a huge burrito and said with his mouth full. "I gave the house and orchard to Aunt Maria and Uncle Carlos. If you want to say something, tell them." He swallowed and took another large bite, savoring the delicious flavors and the moment.

"And we won't sell to anyone! We're moving in tomorrow after I visit the lawyers with Billy," Maria said, feeling freer than ever. "Thank you, Papa, but I'm going to have to ask you to leave. I'll leave your key under the welcome mat once we've left for good," she said, ushering him to the door and closed it behind her.

Don Eduardo sat looking at the door for a long time and said nothing. He took a puff off of his still lit cigar and walked back to his house with his eyes on the dirt road.

TWENTY

HIRO STRIKES OUT

Hiro Nakano, World League Baseball's Most Valuable Player a record eight times in his sixteen years in the game. Homerun and batting champion for ten years and the all-time home-run king with one thousand and forty-two long-balls, walked through the woods like a man incensed.

He was armed enough to take down several large animals and warm enough to survive the coldest of pre-winter nights in Northern California. As he recalled the few trips he and his son had taken over the years he felt even better at Takeshi's chances for survival, even after nearly a week alone in the heavily populated woods.

Takeshi was always an alert and adept student at whatever task he was given to learn. No matter how difficult Hiro would sometimes make it for him, Takeshi would always figure out the best way to accomplish the goal. He had a drive for personal success like no other teen he knew. He was proud of his son and only wished he'd be able to tell him personally.

Hiro walked the same path that was jogged by him and his son hundreds of times over the last few years and tried to get in the mind of his child. "What would I do on my private time if I were Takeshi?" he said to himself.

The leaves on the ground were slippery that morning and Hiro slipped on a frosty patch. A thought shot through his mind and he knew what had happened to his son. "He'd be training!" he said aloud.

Knowing his son's fondness for running, he started off on a light jog on the path. He figured that if he could run the same path as his son, he would see any potential dangers and hopefully find his son.

As he quickened his pace down the same hill Takeshi had fallen, his mind wandered to the image of the blue creature and it's heavy resemblance to his son. "It can't be," he thought and shook his head off of the vision.

Hiro's boot slipped on the same spot that caused his son to tumble forward, but Hiro's great reflexes were still very fast, even for his age of fifty-three years old.

He threw himself to the right and rolled into a large bush and the shrub stopped his body, but Hiro now knew where his son was. He got up, looked down the hill and over the small bridge below. "He's in the ravine!" he yelled in glee. "Takeshi!' he called as loud as he could. "Takeshi! Where are you son?" he listened carefully and heard nothing in return. He called again, "Takeshi!" long and loud, but he heard nothing.

He walked slowly down to the bridge and looked over it carefully as not to fall and saw the many slide markings on the ground and a fallen tree. "He was here!" he shouted and looked around again. "Takeshi!" he called, but no sound came back in return.

Hiro knew his son was close and could not believe it only took him an hour to find his son's trail. "I'm so ashamed," he said and meant it. He knew that if he had shown more courage from the beginning, he might be in his son's company already.

"I can't think like that. It's too late for that. I just have to find him," he said. He walked around the ravine to the fallen tree and saw a torn piece of his son's jump suit caught at the end of a broken branch.

He looked down at the ravine from the new perspective and thought about how difficult it must have been for his son to climb the wet tree so high and steep.

"He made it out alive. That's what matters," he said as he looked around for his son's path, but saw nothing that would give him any indication of his location. He waited for a sign and got it. The great roar of the Sasquatch sang through the air and Hiro's eyes opened wide in worry. The Sasquatch howled again, now only twenty feet ahead of Hiro, but it hid behind trees.

Hiro stood in the open, took out his fifty-caliber pistol and readied it for action. He had some idea of what awaited him, but nothing like the sight that stood in front of him now.

The great beast stood more than twice his height and his shoulders were no less than seven feet wide. White hair covered his entire body and his eyes beamed red at Hiro.

He gnarled and growled loudly, sending ripples of fear through Hiro's body. He stretched his extremely long arms out wide and roared at him, the power of the sound knocking him back and sending him off balance. Hiro righted himself and pointed the gun at the creature, waiting for it to charge.

The Sasquatch ran at Hiro with speed he did not expect from the huge creature. It gave him little time to respond as he fired his gun twice, but unfortunately for him the bullets flew high and wide, just over the Sasquatches right shoulder.

The creature watched the bullets pass its body and zoomed forward at lightning speed toward Hiro sending his huge white hand in an uppercut motion into his chest; killing him on impact. His body flew high in the air and slammed into a huge oak tree. His body stuck between two large branches. The great Hiro Nakano has struck out for the last time.

....

TWENTY-ONE

TAKESHI REACHES OUT

Takeshi ran back into the forest as soon as the Sasquatch opened its eyes and grunted loudly at him. Once he was far enough back to feel comfortable he listened carefully for the footsteps of the creature, but heard none. He felt a little better knowing that it had not tried to harm him again, which meant that there was a possibility for friendship with it He just had to give it some space.

Takeshi looked on the ground around him for mushrooms and found what he was looking for. More in touch with his surroundings, it became easy to find food to eat, but Takeshi's problem was that there wasn't enough of it. He looked at his constantly growing body and wondered how tall he would actually get. He stretched his arm out wide and was dazzled by the brilliant blue color of his skin. "I'm an overgrown papa smurf," he laughed at his own joke. "And I'm gonna need bigger clothes!" he called out and laughed again.

He remembered what happened to him in the little cave when his need for water was great. He had imagined what it would feel like to have the water run down his throat and the water appeared.

Takeshi closed his eyes and imagined himself warmed by the comfort of a light cloth, barely touching his skin, but still providing all the utility he would ever need. He breathed deep and sent the feeling into the Universe. "I have exactly what I need," he whispered aloud.

A tingling mass of energy swirled throughout his body as the feeling grew in him. He breathed again deeply and saw a brilliant white robe settled on him, as light as a feather. He breathed out and knew it to be true.

He opened his eyes and saw a fine-clothed white robe covering his skin and head. "Thank you, Ishmael," he whispered and wished his friend would come to him again.

The light of the forest changed as the air glowed with luminescence. A large bubble appeared in the blink of an eye, as if it had been there the entire time. The mass of energy within the bubble formed into a smile. "How are you, my old friend? You're looking like your old self," said Ishmael.

"Ishmael!" Takeshi said, excited. "I thought I'd never see you again?"

"Oh, do you want me to leave?" he communicated through Takeshi's thoughts.

"No, no, please don't go!" pausing, "You said before that I was beginning to look like my old self?" he said.

"Yes," Ishmael said, still smiling.

"What did you mean?"

"I meant, my dear friend that you are looking like the person that I knew best, a long time ago."

"How did we know each other?" Takeshi asked.

"We were comrades in arms and life."

"What do you mean?"

"I mean that we looked after each other and our families. We were friends that fought side by side and raised our children only a few hundred feet from each other. Until..." Ishmael paused.

"Until what?" Takeshi asked, even more curious.

"Until you made a bad decision," Ishmael's tone was solemn.

"What sort of bad decision?" he was already defensive, but had nothing to direct the feeling.

"We won't go into that right now. You are where you are right now because you have an opportunity to right any wrong you have done in the past. You have made the decision to live out your life's purpose and the purpose of your soul is to act out an even greater act of redemption. You, Takeshi are to go to Tipereth, the land of the Mothertree to protect the Tree of Creation and its fruits of abundance and destruction," said Ishmael.

"Tipereth? Mothertree? Where are they?"

"On the outskirts of the land I occupied for the last nine hundred and twenty-three years. Bubble Valley."

"Bubble Valley?"

"Yes. It exists deep within this Earth and is protected from the destructive people of this land," he said, more solemn.

"How do I get there?"

"You go to Mt. Shasta."

"That's where I am going," Takeshi said, a little defensive.

"You need to move faster and you need to bring someone with you."

Takeshi was startled. "Bring someone with me? Who?" he asked.

"Ru-Ado," said Ishmael and faded away.

"Ru-Ado? Who's Ru-Ado?" he questioned again, but heard the creatures great roar in the distance. Load and vicious enough for him to know that whoever he was yelling at was in deep trouble.

He heard the report of two gunshots and then a great thud. Takeshi's eyes grew wide. "He killed a hunter," he said in horror.

Instinctively, he ducked down low and quickly forgot about his visit from Ishmael. The Sasquatch killed a human; it changed everything about what he thought of it. "I've been treating this thing like he's gonna be my pet. I'm lucky he hasn t killed me. What am I thinking?" he wondered.

Takeshi looked at the position of the sun and took off in the direction of Mt. Shasta. He had a date with destiny that he was no longer able to avoid and was excited about his future.

Later that night he camped cut under a group of trees and was delighted to find out that his robe also protected him from the wind and rain. He slept like a baby on a pile of wet leaves.

That morning he walked up to the river he had been walking parallel to and looked for a place to bathe. He walked into the water and did not feel any of its late November cold, but rather as if it were in mid-July and a perfect temperature.

Takeshi now realized that as long as he wore the robe, he was protected by any outside element. He bathed like a man without care and enjoyed the morning.

After an hour of exploring the area and taking breaks in the water, Takeshi heard the familiar sound of the Sasquatch coming in his direction. He put the hood of the robe over his head and walked into the vegetation.

The Sasquatch stood in the open and smelled the air. He had the confused look of someone who had misinterpreted one of his moves. Takeshi remained motionless and quiet. He smiled knowing now that the robe also protected him from detection through smell. He thought, "This gets cooler and cooler," and peered closer.

The Bigfoot walked towards the river and away from Takeshi's sight. He knew it was time to stop being afraid. "Even though he's a man killer," he said under his breath.

That night Takeshi stayed in his little oasis and listened for any sound of the Sasquatch when he had a thought. "What if I call him? How crazy is that?" He paused and knew it was the only thing that would cure his particular itch of curiosity.

He took a deep breath and bellowed into the air, just as he had remembered the creature doing. He heard no response. He looked to the ground and picked up a stick. He banged it on the tree in front of him three times and roared again, long and louder than before. He thought, "Wow, that felt great," and waited for a response.

A roar came back at him, it was the creature, and he knew it. Takeshi roared again, exactly like before. The creature roared back, but not as loud.

Takeshi took a chance and yelled out in a gruff Japanese, "Who are you?"

He heard nothing in return, but tried again. "Who are you?" his voice was now hoarse with overuse.

Then he heard it, "Ru-Ado..." ong and loud. "I am Ru-Ado!" said the creature. The Sasquatch was the person Ishmael had told him of and he was glad for it.

TWENTY-TWO

....

A SILENT SO-LONG

Caytoe lay in his bed awake with his eyes closed. The sun still had a little time to wait before it peeked over the horizon and the birds camped in trees outside his window cheeped impatiently for need to fill their bellies.

He heard Hathor jump from the floor onto his breakfast table and knew the day was about to begin, but wanted to spend a few extra minutes in bed.

Though he was in great physical shape, his body was stiff from several days of meditation. He knew that the pain would go away once he got up and stretched, but getting up to do it was a chore in itself. He thought about the last few days and marveled at the sequence of events that were unfurling in front of him.

He recalled watching the old giant's death and then the younger, running up to his elder and falling on top of him once he touched the poisonous vines. As soon as he heard the name of the fallen warrior, Tem, he knew why he was there and what was needed of him. The only task that lay ahead was telling Billy. Teaching him what was necessary would come with ease once he knew the boy's commitment.

Caytoe opened his eyes and heard the demanding mew of Hathor. "Yes, my lord, I'll be right there," he said in with an old English accent.

"Don't mock me, Caytoe," Hathor mewed from the other room.

"Alright, alright. Always so sensitive." Caytoe laughed and got out of bed, ignoring the pain. He opened a can of food and emptied the contents into Hathor's bowl. "This is gonna have to do for the day, alright?" Caytoe asked his friend, but was only given a cursory glance before diving into his morning meal. "It wouldn't hurt you to catch a mouse or two on your own from time to time, you know, he said as he watched the cat eat silently for a few moments before getting annoyed, "I'm not going to get through to you, I see, but I'm going to be busy all day with the boy. Eat up ole' buddy," he said, scratched the cat on the head and walked out the front door into the garden.

Caytoe looked up and saw cloudless blue skies and knew it was going to be a perfect day. He breathed in deep and smelled the many blossoms around him. A mild breeze passed over his body and he smiled in thanks.

Caytoe looked to the ground and saw that it was wet from a nighttime shower. "That sure makes things easy today," he said and walked over to his large herb garden. "Let me at least get some of you herbs hung to dry before the boy comes," he said. He walked over to his work shed and back with a scissor and pruning shears that he used to take long clippings from each of his many herbs.

He picked three different kinds of basil, dill weed, oregano, rosemary, thyme, and spearmint, lavender and white sage. By the time he was done two hours later, he had fifty intricately tied bundles of herbs to be dried. He walked to the back of his work shed where he had a wheel barrow leaning up against the wall. He let the barrow fall, walked it over to the herbs and filled it high.

Caytoe then walked the barrow to his front porch, which was screened in and protected from the rain. He had a lonely chair in the corner of the room, but a tower of abandoned plant containers occupied it. On the ceiling was a complicated system of wires designed to mimic a spider's web and clothespins hung in wait all over the room.

Caytoe got to work straight away and hung them all in less than a half-hour. He stepped outside of his porch and admired the day's harvest. He breathed deep and dug his bare feet into the moist soil, loving the feel.

Caytoe almost never wore shoes of any kind and if he absolutely had to, he wore sandals for a short time only. Caytoe knew his connection to the Earth and felt empty without it.

A growl came from deep within and he knew he had to eat something soon. He walked into his kitchen and removed a cloth from a large metal colander, revealing a bouquet of perfectly grown vegetable sprouts.

He picked up a spray bottle that sat behind the colander and watered the sprouts well before grabbing many small handfuls of the micro-greens to eat. He loved the spicy flavors and the quick energy it brought to his day.

When he had his fill he covered the colander with the cloth and had several large glasses of water from a pitcher filled with lemon quarters and spearmint sprigs. He smacked his lips and felt his energy growing by the second.

"Knock, knock, knock!" came a sound tapping at his door. Caytoe saw a smiling Billy and knew he had made his decision. Caytoe walked to the door and said to himself, "Let's get to work." He was glad to be in this boy's service.

Later on that day once Caytoe had made Billy feel at home and had him taste several of the fruits in his garden, he asked, "Is everything taken care of at home?" and ushered him out of the garden towards the grapevine labyrinth.

"Sure is. Aunt Maria took me to see the lawyer's yesterday. I had to sign a few papers and then we were gone," Billy said without care. "Everyone's really happy, except..." he hesitated.

"You," said Caytoe.

"Yeah. Ever since I saw my parents through the castle window, I've wanted nothing more than to be there with them. Can I do that? Can I live in Bubble Valley with my other self?" he asked.

"No, you cannot, but there is another way," said Caytoe.

"There is?"

"Yes. The young man who is the son of your parents has gone into a deep coma..." he paused, "...and sadly, there is no way he could recover from his injury."

"I'm confused. What does that mean for me?" asked Billy.

"Well, that means you can do a good deed for both of you by agreeing to switch bodies with each other," he said a bit uneasy.

"Switch bodies?" Billy gasped.

"Yes, it is possible," said Caytoe.

"How?"

"Well, that's a little complicated on my end, but for you it's merely an agreement with yourself," Caytoe said, very serious.

"An agreement with myself?"

"Yes. An agreement about what you are willing to believe."

"About what?"

"About which world you live in. All you need do is believe that you are Tem and I will do the rest," he said.

232

"What do you need to do?"

"I need to convince the greatest warrior of all-time that his only chance for survival is to take the body of an undersized twelve year old boy," Caytoe smirked and Billy looked at him uneasily. "It'll be OK, don't worry, I'll talk to him tonight. In the mean time I want you to say your good-byes to your family in your own way, but don't tell them what you are planning to do." Caytoe was grim with his words. "Silence is the most important tool you have. The Universe is listening to everything you say and will test you when you least expect it. Especially when you taunt it," he said.

"OK," said Billy.

"In their eyes nothing will have changed. You will still come back to them after your evening visit, but just in body. The person inside that body will be Tem."

"Are you going to prepare him too?" Billy asked.

Caytoe looked away from the boy for the first time and said, "I'm going to try."

A little later on Billy walked in the front door of Maria's house and saw nothing, but a bunch of blurs streaking through the hallways, carrying large boxes from room to room. Maria dictated the whole process for the family from the middle of the living room. "You two stay out of the boxes of clothes. You don't want me to have to fold them all again," she chastised her girls. "Manny, go help your father take apart our bed upstairs. He refuses to believe that he needs to use tools to get it done." She tossed a bag in the air to him as he walked to her and Manny caught it without thinking. "Take these up to your father and make sure he uses them. I'm glad he stopped drinking, but I need to make sure he doesn't break all of the furniture at the same time," she said, very happy.

"Yes, Mom," was all Manny managed before running up the stairs to do as he was told. Everyone in the house was excited and Billy was glad to be the one to bring them all so much joy and purpose.

Aunt Maria saw Billy standing in the doorway looking in and knew what he was feeling. "You're a good boy, Billy. Your mother would be proud of you," she said, but Billy said nothing in return. He smiled big. "I'm going to see my mother tomorrow," he thought and walked over to her and gave her a hug. "Thanks for all you've done for me since I've come. It's been nice to know that someone cares," he said with sincerity.

"Aw, such a sweet boy," she said and squeezed his cheeks. It was the only thing he disliked about his Aunt Maria. It seemed like every time he turned around, there she was with her iron-like fingers, likely from picking tangerines her entire life. She would latch on with her stubby little fingers and squeeze his cheeks, always leaving a mark.

"Aunt Maria, not the cheeks!" Billy laughed and ran away from her clutches to his bedroom upstairs. He looked at his bag of clothes and few books and saw the entirety of his possessions. "Not leaving much behind, am I?" he said and left the room to watch Manny calm Uncle Carlos down after stubbing his toes on the corner of the wooden bed frame. He then snuck off down the stairs and out of the screen door, this time avoiding Aunt Maria and her vice-grip fingers.

He walked near his grandfather's home and looked to see if the old man was looking out of the window. If there was one time he felt like he could say good-bye to someone who never cared it was this one, but the doorway was empty; Don Eduardo was nowhere in sight.

Billy thought, "Just as well," exactly like his mother had done a thousand times before him. He walked down the dirt road like a man with a purpose and thought, "If Tem is as large as my parents then I'm gonna be huge," he looked down, "Good-Bye little legs. Good-Bye little arms and fingers and toes." He wiggled his fingers around and tried to imagine what it would be like to be a giant.

The thought was so foreign to him that it was hard to process, but so much had happened to him in such a little time that it was all one big blur. He walked up to his Aunt Maria's new orchard and smiled at the beauty of the land. Though the vegetation around the trees had over grown a bit, there was no doubt that the tangerine trees were in their full glory. Hundreds upon thousands of ripening tangerines scattered the trees. He knew that his family and Tem would be taken care of. He didn't want to look at the house in the middle of the orchard, because there was no reason. "Let Tem see it first," he said and walked to Mr. Caytoe's house in silence. Before he had a chance to answer the door, Caytoe popped in the doorway. "Are you ready to take a ride?" he said in a funny voice.

Billy was startled, but laughed out loud.

238

TWENTY-THREE

....

THE MOTHERTREE

Ru-Ado sat in his cave and thought about the dead human and his thunder-stick. The vision of the broken man in the tree wouldn't leave his mind simply because the human looked so much like the zuzuans, just much smaller and without hair on their bodies. It made him ill to think of killing one of his own and the death of the human was little different. He wanted to go back and take the human down from the tree to bring it back to the Earth, but knew where there was one human, another was sure to be not far behind.

Ru-Ado recalled the wind that passed his shoulder after the man fired his weapon at him and the fear of it woke up in him. He struck the man on pure instinct and had to live with his choice. He also knew it wouldn't be the last time he would have to make such a choice.

Ru-Ado looked at his wound and saw that it had completely healed; only a minor soreness was present when he touched the scar. He needed to eat, but was weary of any further human presence in the forest. It only took a few more minutes to change his mind once he thought of the easy meal the fish trap brought.

Like all zuzuan warriors, Ru-Ado knew how to sneak through the forest in constant evasion from any of its potential threats, but Ru-Ado had learned to take it to another level, especially in the winter and heavy white snow covered the ground. His white hair blended in, making him nearly invisible.

On days when snow wasn't present, Ru-Ado learned to look for anything around him to blend in with. As children, the zuzuans were told to go into the forest to find prey on their own by only camouflaging their existence. Not an easy task for anyone, but by the time the young zuzuans had seen seven winters, they would be masters at deception.

Ru-Ado skulked through the woods, masking his presence until he made it to the river. He looked at the sky for any more metal birds and saw none. Ru-Ado knew it was time for him to leave this land and head to the Sacred Grounds. His father, Ado-Han would be close-by now and very tired from the journey. He wished he would have been able to catch up with him sooner, but he knew it was not possible. He would leave in the evening, but first would eat the incredible gift of six river trout back n his cave and sleep again.

He ate the fish while sitting cn the log he used as the trap and looked into the sky. There was so much that he did not know about the world he sought power in. He wanted knowledge, but had no way of getting it at the moment.

Though he tried to block the thought, "You will be the Zo-Han," the voice of the spirt rang through his head. "Of course I will be the Zo-Han, but I will not have it given to me. I will seek the man in the white robe from my dream and follow him to my destiny. I will no longer feel afraid in my own land. I will hide for no one!" he bellowed out. His words were strong and resolute.

At that moment a metal bird flew out from the trees and hovered above him. Ru-Ado roared in anger, but the bird did not move. He ooked to the log and saw the stone he had set aside, picked it up and hurled it at the bird with incredible speed. The stone hit squarely, the bird fell into the river and floated towards Ru-Ado. He reached out and picked it up before it sailed with the water's flow and looked at it. There was no soul in this creature. He saw a red light flicker on and off as he crushed it with his enormous hands and threw it back into the river, watching the pieces float away.

Then he heard it, a howl completely foreign, but still vaguely familiar. There was silence and then the howl came again, but much longer. Ru-Ado knew that this creature had to be nearly as large as him to sing such a long song. He called back, curious, but strong. His voice sent any animals in the area quickly out of sight.

He listened and heard the call again, louder and longer than before. He was impressed by the power it gave off. He now knew it wasn't a zuzuan, but an animal that knew off the zuzuan people. Ru-Ado called back, this time a little less intimidating to let the animal know that he wasn't presenting a threat.

The unknown beast called out again, but this time there were words. The language sounded like zuzuan, but was not. The beast called out again, repeated the words and he understood. It asked him what he was called. Ru-Ado's heart sang as he called out in return, "Ru-Ado! I am Ru-Ado!" he said and it felt good for him to hear his name out loud.

The creature hesitated, "I am Takeshi! Will you allow me to show myself?" it cried.

"Takeshi!" Ru-Ado mimicked, "Walk forward and show yourself. I will not harm you," he said as he waited. In a moment Ru-Ado was staring at the sight he'd been waiting for. It was the man in the white robe. He stood before Ru-Ado without fear. "Hello, Ru-Ado," he said.

"Hello, Takeshi," Ru-Ado said and bowed his head to his new friend who stood a full foot taller than him.

Takeshi smiled and bowed back to the giant in front of him.

"I saw you in my dreams," he said.

"I saw you," Takeshi said in return.

Ru-Ado reached out to touch Takeshi's robes and felt the material. It felt as soft as rabbit fur, but very light.

"It is called a robe," said Takeshi. It protects me from the cold," he said and opened his robe to him. "I do not have hair like you," he showed.

Ru-Ado looked at Takeshi's body and thought. "You are the human from the hole in the Earth," everything now making sense to him. He liked this human and would be glad to call him a friend.

"Thank you for my life," said Takeshi and bowed again to him.

"You do not look the same," said Ru-Ado.

"There were many changes. Some I understand and many I do not," Takeshi responded.

"You do not smell like a human any longer."

"I don't think that I am. I am Takeshi, that is all that matters to me."

"I am Ru-Ado," he said with confidence and meant the same.

"Ru-Ado, I am leaving for the great mountain ahead in the morning. I was shown an entrance in."

"I will follow you, but I will leave you at our Sacred Grounds. I have to see my father and say good-bye," said Ru-Ado.

"I will wait for you," Takeshi said and extended a large blue hand to Ru-Ado. Ru-Ado looked at him with bewilderment, but quickly saw what was wanted of him and took hold of his hand. His huge white hand contrasted against the color of Takeshi's blue skin.

Ru-Ado and Takeshi walked out of the forest and saw the base of Mount Shasta. Even though they now knew how to talk to each other, it seemed they didn't need to. Both were silent for their own reasons.

Ru-Ado knew in his heart that he would see his father today and did not know how that was going to turn out. Even if he asked Ru-Ado to come back to the tribe he knew he couldn't. His destiny was at his fingertips and he was only looking forward to whatever that might be. He looked to his new friend and was grateful for their common bond of wanting a new experience. Ru-Ado had never had any friends outside of his tribe, but he still trusted him. That evening he left Takeshi without word to find Ado-Han, but found him at the base of the mountain by sunrise. What he needed to do didn't take as long as he thought it might, but he was happy with the results. He knew he would see his family again one day but it would be as Zo-Han. He never told Takeshi what had happened between him and his father, but would someday. He had to see what Takeshi was truly capable of. Not all trust could be earned at once.

Takeshi's mind tried to focus on something beyond the immense stonewall in front of him, but he could not see. This disturbed him only a little, because in his heart of hearts he knew what lay ahead. He saw

Ru-Ado walk off on his own and left him alone to do as he needed. It wasn't his business to know and he would respect his need for privacy.

He walked a long time towards the base of the mountain and reached it before sun-up. A single solid slab of stone stood in front of him, larger than a baseball diamond. Takeshi scanned the enormous rock and saw a hieroglyph of a large spiral and knew he was in the right place. He looked back and saw Ru-Ado walk up to him. They looked at each other and didn't need to share words. Ru-Ado was there and ready.

Takeshi looked up at the slab and immediately knew what to do. He imagined himself and Ru-Ado walking through the solid stone without harm or injury. He saw them walking side by side and into another forest, much larger than his own. He felt the warmth of the sun and the coolness of the air in a treasure of a land.

He looked back to Ru-Ado and said, "To whatever awaits," and Ru-Ado nodded in agreement, following Takeshi through the stone and into a land he could not imagine even in dreams. A forest twenty times bigger than anything they had ever seen stood in front of them, with strange flowers and plants everywhere.

A gigantic tree that looked as old as time stood in front of it all and the sweet voice of a woman rang through their souls. "Welcome, sons of Tipereth. I'm glad you are home," said the voice as they looked at each other with wonder in their eyes.

TWENTY-FOUR

....

NEW EYES

Tem hovered over his body in absolute wonder. He saw his parents crying next to his body, but couldn't understand why. His friend, Chica perched solemnly on his chest, not moving from him no matter the chaos that went on around him.

Ishmael's body lay next to him on a large bed of pillows. Several ancient looking women knelt next to him with their heads down. His face carried a light smile, as if he were grateful for a needed rest.

Tem's soldiers paced the corridors of the castle with unbridled anger, not knowing where to show their frustration. The Captain said there was nothing they could do about a poisonous plant. It was Tem's foolish move that put him in a coma. It was their job to protect the castle from invaders.

As soon as the word throughout the land had spread that the Anak Tribe's greatest warrior had fallen, he knew there would be insurrection. The Anak Tribe had held power over Bubble Valley for the last twenty-five years and the people wanted change.

Now with Tem out of the picture, there would be no great competition in the coming Bubble Valley games and the sea of power would shift to another tribe.

Tensions were high in the castle and on the entire pyramid, as it seemed every citizen of Bubble Valley was outside talking to their neighbors about the fallen warrior and games-man.

"Why are you crying? I am not dead nor am I ready to die," Tem called out to his parents and Chica.

From behind him Caytoe called out, "You are in a deep sleep. Your body will never be able to recover from the amount of poison you received from the vine," he said gravely.

Tem turned around. "Who are you? What do you know?" he said in confusion.

"My name is Caytoe and I am a friend."

"You are no friend I know," Tem said in anger.

"No, but I know you in another form and in another place."

"What place?" Tem balked

"The place of your dreams."

"What do you know of my dreams?"

"*I know* that in the world we are friends, you are a twelve year old boy."

"Are you mad?" Tem stammered.

Caytoe laughed. "Maybe, but I speak truth. In this other world your parents have just died a tragic death and your only wish is to live among them again."

"Who is this boy?" Tem questioned.

"He is you."

"Me?"

"Yes and he is you, just a different aspect of you that wants a different set of experiences. We are powerful people with the ability to do anything we wish."

Tem looked at him deeply and said, "OK, let's say I believe you. How does this help *him*?" he pointed to his body below.

"It helps him by providing that amazing body a chance to do good and give a child a gift he thought to never have. It helps you because you will never step into that body again. The only way you will be able to live out the remainder of this experience is to do it in the child's body."

251

"Switch bodies?" Tem gasped.

"Yes! It's the only way," Caytoe said as a fact.

"How do you know all of this?" Tem shot back. "Are you a demon? Do you do Nas-Tak's bidding?" he said, ready to battle.

"I am no demon. I am dedicated to good for others. My only gift is that I am able to walk two worlds and carry the same mind. Otherwise I am just a friend who knows how to help when it is needed most," Caytoe said simply.

Tem looked at him a long time, then to himself below. "When can we do it?" he said and looked longingly at parents and friends he would never see again.

Billy sat in a comfortable chair in the center of Caytoe's little shed in the middle of his grapevine maze and breathed deeply. Caytoe sat behind him in a small wooden chair doing the same.

After several minutes they each felt the familiar vibrations, lifted out of their bodies and floated just above. Caytoe looked in the vapor for something, but did not see it. He thought of a large open field in the mid-west, which had a long wooden cattle fence. Tem stood on one side and he and Billy on the other.

252

In a moment they were each there, smelling the damp air after a rain.

Tem stood high above the fence and waited patiently.

Billy looked up and could not get over the size of the man that he was to become. He could only stare with his mouth open.

Caytoe spoke up, "We make an agreement between two halves of the same soul." He looked to Billy. "William Augustin Waters." He looked to Tem, "Tem of the Anak Tribe," he paused, "once you both cross this fence, there will be no return." William will be Tem and Tem, William. We ask the Archangels for love and compassion in this time of great transition. We love and respect the power of the Universe," he paused again. "Please cross the fence," he said to them both and watched Billy step through a wide door and Tem step over the fence.

"William, when you wake up, you will be Tem of the Anak Tribe. You are the pride of your people. Learn fast and remain strong. Tem, when you wake up you will be William Augustin Waters, an orphaned son and lost soul. You must bring your strength, honor and courage into his frail body. Live with valor, the people need you." He nodded his head and was gone from the field.

Billy and Tem looked at each other briefly and heard "Wake up!"

Tem opened his eyes and saw Caytoe looking at him. He smiled, until he saw the size of his hands. He screamed as loud as his little lungs would allow.

Caytoe laughed.

Billy woke to his mother and father's huge figures hovering above him with tears running down their face. Billy smiled as Billy for the last time.

ABOUT THE AUTHOR

C.C. Corry is an award winning writer, dedicated dad and an avid lover of nature. He lives in Fern Park, Florida with his future wife, younger son and seven happy cats.